Ride The Stone Pony

RIDE THE STONE PONY

RUSS BUBAS

Merrimack Media
Boston, Massachusetts

ISBN: print: 978-1-945756-01-6

ISBN: ebook: 978-1-945756-03-0

Published by Merrimack Media, Boston, Massachusetts 2018

Chapter 1

"**D**an!" Brian from Ace Plumbing nearly was shouting into the phone. "I think I need you."

His voice was dripping with urgency and frayed nerves.

"Oh, hi Brian." Still husky from sleep. "I was hoping for a call from a supermodel, but I get one from a plumber instead."

"I think my assistant manager is stealing from me. Not sure, but it looks bad."

"Things being flushed away?"

Silence on the other end.

"Sorry, it's still early for me."

"My assistant manager comes on today at three o'clock. Can you get here?"

Dan Hughes checked the time: 8 a.m. "Yeah, I'll see you there."

"Thanks, Dan. Appreciate it." He hung up.

Hughes walked to the window in his shorts and watched the worker-bee traffic on Beacon Street. He stretched and padded to the kitchen to make coffee. Whenever he had a cup of hot Starbucks coffee, he sat at his desk and thought about things. Seemed like he just moved from crisis to crisis, a spinning wheel. He considered it with a dose of melancholy, then figured he did it to himself—a cure for boredom. After two coffees and a large bowl of cereal with fresh blueberries, he finally felt alive and more like a private eye. Then he pulled on a new tee shirt, shorts, and well-worn sneakers and headed out and down Tremont Street to LA Fitness.

He checked in and worked the circuit. An hour later, he was soaked and felt great. He took some minutes to admire the female "talent" in the club. The warm summer day lent to some abbreviated attire, so he did another twenty minutes. By noon, he was back in the shower in his apartment, getting ready to head to the plumbing supply house an hour away in Fall River.

He dressed in tan slacks and a crisp white shirt. He always wore a power red tie for interrogations and paired it with his lightweight navy blazer. That was his summer staple. His Tumi briefcase was ready to go, and he slid his Airweight .38 onto his belt, out of sight. After locking up the apartment behind him, he walked to his parked Miata on the street.

Fall River, the hometown of Lizzie Borden, grew tired with sagging shoulders but was involved now in a hopeful rebirth. Even the waterfront was being polished up, attracting a more upscale crowd than the usual shot-and-beer clientele.

Hughes cruised just above the speed limit down Route 24, listening to the tuned pitch of the two-seater's twin pipes. He wanted to arrive just before his subject showed up for the three o'clock shift so he could get briefed and set up. As it turned out, he was early, so he slowly rolled down the street, past used car lots, freestanding bars, and an occasional massage parlor, to eyeball the operation and get a feel for it. The air was summer-still and smelled of car exhaust and seaweed.

After two drive-bys, he pulled into the large parking lot behind Ace Plumbing's main building and parked discreetly in the corner. Off to the left of the lot, there were two white delivery box trucks parked in front of what appeared to be the warehouse. A couple of plain sedans were parked adjacent to what looked like the rear door to the showroom. He sat in the car, unnoticed, pulled open his briefcase, and reviewed the notes that had been emailed to him.

Apparently, the counterman, who was also the assistant manager, was not reporting some sales. There were gaps in the sequence of the sales slips, and a number of them were missing. It was assumed these were cash sales, as the percentage of cash to charges had slipped down. The problem was twofold. First, he was not the only one working the counter and, second, he had been employed for over six years.

Hughes shook his head. No real proof, yet it was another case where they expected miracles. He closed his briefcase and headed inside through the rear door. Inside was a short hallway leading to the front showroom and parts counter. There was one customer at the counter talking to an employee wearing a blue uniform shirt. Off to the right was an office semi-enclosed in glass. Hughes could see a man in a white shirt talking on the phone behind a desk. The boss, he assumed. He looked startled when Hughes knocked.

He was a big man, probably a college football lineman in his younger days, now carrying a gut the size of a beer keg. He got up and offered Hughes a hand the size of a catcher's mitt.

"You're Dan Hughes. Come in," he said. "Brian told me you'd be coming. Bob Hurley here. Hope you can straighten this out. I've been up at night for the past two weeks worrying about it."

"I'll see what I can do," Hughes replied, gesturing to a chair in front of the desk that he then occupied. "What's going on, do you think?"

"I've got this counter guy, an assistant manager really, working here for the past six years. Name is Joe Koslowski. Doing a great job."

"And?" Hughes said.

"My accountant upgraded our software, and I can now get a printout of the cash-to-charge sales ratio. I noticed the percentage of cash-to-charge sales seems to be going down. No reason for it. So I took a look at our manual sales slips, and some seem to be missing. Hard to tell because each counterman has his own book of receipts, so hard to keep any kind of sequence."

"So, you suspect you have a partner in the profits? How long has the difference between cash to charges been going on?"

"Don't really know. The software was just installed a month ago, so I don't know what was going on before that." Hurley fidgeted with a pencil in his strawberry-colored hands.

Hughes thought for a minute. "Why do you suspect Mr. Koslowski?"

"He's been going through an ugly divorce. Heard his wife caught him feeding in the henhouse. And about a month ago or so, he showed up with a new Ford F-150 truck. Even had a chrome side rail. And a customer came in last week for a refund, and we couldn't find any record of the sale. From his description of the salesperson, it has to be Joe. It was for three hundred bucks. Had to give the guy the money."

Hughes made a note of that on his legal pad. "Does Joe know you suspect him or that I'm coming in?"

"No, Brian told me not to say anything, so I didn't." Hurley shrugged. "Joe should be arriving in the next ten minutes or so."

"OK," Hughes said, standing. "OK to use this office?"

"Sure." Then a rumble from outside as a dark-blue pickup truck went by the front windows. Hurley looked startled. "Here he is."

"OK, "Hughes said. "I'll be here. Just tell him someone wants to see him in the office. Don't tell him who or why. I need the initiative. Do you have any sales receipts? I could use a stack of them."

"Top drawer. I'll get him when he walks in," Hurley replied, sounding worried. He then left the office. Hughes opened his notepad, took out some file folders, and found a pile of wrinkled sales receipts in the desk drawer. He put them on the desk next to his briefcase. He stood behind the desk, aimlessly shuffling the papers, as Hurley led Joe Koslowski in. Hughes continued to shuffle papers like he was looking for something important.

"Thanks, Bob," he said, glancing up and gesturing to the chair in front of the desk for Koslowski to sit. Still standing, he looked directly and blankly at Koslowski and saw a fortyish, wiry man with thinning hair and a scar across his right cheek. He was dressed in a company polo shirt and khakis that looked like they were slightly too small. Koslowski looked left and right, clearly unaccustomed to seeing a man in a dark jacket, white shirt, and red tie in the plumbing supply shop. Hughes saw a slight nervous tic in Koslowski's left eye and thought, *Gotcha!*

Koslowski started to ask what the meeting was about. Hughes stopped him by putting one hand up while still looking down at his papers. Finally, he sat and said, "Joe, what priors do you have?"

Koslowski, clearly confused, looked blankly at Hughes, but as he thought through the question, he then got it. "Uh, I got charged with assault years ago, but it was a trumped-up charge."

"How many years ago?" Hughes asked.

"I don't know, maybe five or six."

"What did they do to you?" Hughes wrote some gibberish in his notepad without looking up.

"Uh, I got probation, but it's finished now."

Hughes looked up from his pad and stared directly into Koslowski's eyes. He was quiet for a minute, watching Koslowski becoming more nervous. Then he said loudly, "Joe, the next five minutes here may affect the rest of your life. It's critical you are completely honest with me. I'm a private investigator and you are not under arrest at this time."

The color from Koslowski's face drained like wine being poured from a bottle. He shifted in his chair and glanced out the window. He was quiet.

Hughes said, "Joe, look at me. You won't believe it, but I'm the best friend you can have at this time. I am not looking to blow anything out of proportion, but I will not tolerate any lies."

Koslowski's mouth opened slightly, but nothing came out immediately. Then he said, "I have no idea what you are talking about." His body language said something entirely different, Hughes noted. He was now sure the boss's suspicions were accurate.

"OK, Joe, you've been taking cash payments from customers for yourself," Hughes said, careful not to use the words "stealing" and "theft."

"There probably is a reason you did this," Hughes went on. "You can tell me or not, I don't care, but I'll listen. I have three things that have to happen to straighten this out. You have to be totally honest with me, you have to apologize to the boss, and you have to try to make it right." And before Koslowski had a chance to think about it, Hughes said, "How well do you get along with Bob?"

After a second, Koslowski said, "OK, I guess. But I haven't done anything."

"Joe, you are violating the very first rule: don't lie to me. My job is to straighten things out, not hurt anyone, but if I have to, I can bring criminal charges against anyone involved." Hughes softened his tone and leaned a little forward. He watched as Koslowski's thought process went into overdrive. He was chewing on his options.

Silent for a full minute, Koslowski finally said, "Maybe once or twice I made a mistake and didn't ring up some sales. But it only happened once, maybe twice."

With that admission, Hughes knew it was now only a matter of time to get to the truth. "Joe, please, there has been a very extensive investigation going on. Tell me the first time you didn't ring up a sale. Was it more than two years ago like we believe?"

Koslowski looked startled. "Two years? No way."

Hughes smiled to himself. *A matter of time now.*

He changed his tone; now it was quieter and soothing. "Joe, you don't seem like a criminal to me. Maybe you've made some mistakes. They can either ruin your life or we can try to get this straightened out."

Koslowski was silent, thinking.

Hughes gave him a minute, then said, "When was the first time you did it?" Again, he avoided words like "stealing" and "theft."

Koslowski said nothing, just stared blankly at the wall.

Hughes said, "Joe, an internal audit indicates you took about ten thousand dollars."

He looked startled. "Not that much," he finally said.

"Yes, that much. You probably don't even know how much. Do you have a dependency problem?"

"What?"

"Are you addicted to dope? Gambling?"

"No, I play the lottery. Maybe too much, but I don't think I have a problem."

Hughes looked sympathetic. "Joe, if you want to tell me why you took the money, I'll listen. But I really don't care. Remember the three things: the whole truth, an apology, and to try to make it right."

"I," he started, then stopped. Then, "I needed money for my divorce. Then, I dunno know, I guess it seemed easy."

"When was your divorce?" Hughes asked quietly.

Koslowski thought for a minute. "I guess almost two years ago."

Hughes wrote in his notebook. He seemed to be studying something. "OK, maybe ten thousand is right?" Hughes threw the number out to get his attention but didn't think it would fly.

Koslowski didn't answer at first. His head dropped and he almost whispered, "I guess so."

"Who else is taking money or merchandise?"

"No one that I know of." He was a caldron of remorse, humiliation, and fear.

Hughes took his notebook and started writing out the confession. When he was done, it spelled out how Koslowski was taking cash sales by destroying sales slips and was admitting he took at least ten thousand dollars. He stood up and walked around the desk and said, "My handwriting is not so good, so I'll read this with you."

Koslowski was shaking slightly. He nodded and went along as Hughes read him the statement. "Is this the truth?" Hughes asked.

Koslowski nodded and Hughes told him where to sign and initial the corrections. He then said, "Wait here. I'm going to get Bob and you need to tell him what's been going on." He walked out, closing the door behind him, and signaled to Hurley, who was standing expectedly across the showroom.

"What happened?" he asked.

"I got a statement for ten thousand dollars. It may be more, but I don't think he can remember how many times he stole. It goes back almost two years."

Hurley was stunned. "What? Ten thousand dollars?"

"Could be more," Hughes said.

"Dear God," Hurley mumbled. "What now?"

I need you to come in and listen to his admissions. Then you have to make a decision about what you are going to do. I don't know if he has the money to pay you back, but I would go for restitution first."

They walked back into the office together. Koslowski was staring out the window at a nearly empty parking lot. He looked up to Hurley and shook his head. "Sorry," he mumbled almost to himself.

Hughes immediately jumped in. "Bob, as you know, we

have been doing an extensive investigation here. This man has been collecting cash from customers and keeping it himself. Joe, tell Mr. Hurley what's been going on."

"Bob, I'm sorry." His voice was shaky. "I let you down. I don't know why except my divorce cost a lot and took a lot out of me. I'm really sorry."

Hurley glared at him. "Joe, we were good to you. Gave you raises and supported you throughout. How could you steal from us?"

Koslowski hung his head. Hughes jumped in again. "Joe signed a statement admitting he took at least ten thousand dollars." He showed the statement to Hurley and asked, "Joe, is this the truth? Is this your signature?"

Koslowski nodded.

Hughes turned to Hurley. "You have some decisions to make. This man can be criminally prosecuted if you want to bring charges. I think he should pay you back all that he took. But, understand, if he pays back full restitution, the courts will not be particularly interested in bringing charges. But you don't have to make that decision now. Maybe give Joe a chance to bring in the ten thousand."

Hurley glared at Koslowski. "Joe, will you give back the money?"

"I'll try. But I don't know where I'll get it."

Once again, Hughes took control of the situation. "Bob, give him a week to come up with the money. If he brings it in, you can take that into account. But don't accept payments. All or nothing."

Hurley said, "OK, I'll wait to see if you will do the right thing."

Hughes said, "Joe, get whatever personal effects you have and get out of here. Thank Mr. Hurley for giving you a break and not having you led out of here in handcuffs."

Koslowski got up slowly. "Sorry, Mr. Hurley." Then he turned to Hughes and stuck out his hand and said, "Thank you."

Hughes nodded.

Koslowski then shuffled out like he was going to a funeral.

Hughes started putting his files together and into his briefcase. "I'll send you a report with a copy of his statement. If he doesn't come back with the money, you may wish to ask for a show-cause hearing for a complaint to be issued. Then let the courts collect the restitution for you."

Hurley was as pale as cream. "Thanks, Dan, I guess. This has been quite a shock. I never would have believed it."

"Glad to help. Call if you need me again." He started for the back door as Hurley looked back at the rest of his staff.

Chapter 2

As Hughes stepped out into the back lot, he scanned left and right to see if Koslowski got a feeling of revenge. All clear.

The light was waning as the day started losing its strength and heat. Hughes walked quickly to the Miata. He got in, looked left and right again, and turned the key to the satisfying sound he loved. He drove slowly out and onto the street, still alert, anticipating an angry Koslowski.

Fall River receded away behind him like a strange land as he headed for Route 24 North. Hughes thought about Joe Koslowski and how close he came to ruining his life. He figured Hurley would ask for the money, and if it were not forthcoming, he eventually would let it disappear behind the stress of trying to run his business. Koslowski probably would go on as though nothing had happened. But Hughes did his job with very little evidence. He let the Miata open up a little in the fast lane, and it settled in at an easy seventy-five miles, shimmering in the August heat.

Hughes motored back to Boston, the adrenaline still flowing hard through his body. Thinking he was on a roll, he decided to work the workman's comp fraud case that had been hanging around for a couple of weeks. Had to catch the guy cheating by claiming his back was out when it wasn't. He parked the Miata at a meter on Beacon Street and walked up to his apartment on Joy Street. A quick change into jeans, grabbing a can of tuna fish, and he headed to the hinterlands west of the city.

It was dusk and he was onto something. He saw the subject get into his car with a baseball bat and glove. He was following him hard. The Miata's engine was screeching like nails on a blackboard. The subject he was tailing was in his peripheral vision on a parallel road to his left. He tried a hard turn onto a loose gravel connector that came up fast, sliding into a pothole that seemed as deep as a Florida sinkhole. There was a loud bang as the right tie rod broke and the little sports car skidded into a ditch, spewing clouds of dust and knocking him against the steering wheel almost senseless. Sitting motionless, he let the dizziness fade before climbing out of the car. He stood, peered down the road, and shrugged.

There goes this surveillance, he thought to himself as he looked stupidly at the wheel folded under the car like a fat serving tray. Looking around, he saw no help in sight, just traffic occasionally speeding by him with indifference. He kneeled in the gravel and peered under the car. Looked bad. Getting up, he dusted off his pants, shook his head, and pulled out his cell phone. The tow truck took an hour to arrive; when it did, the driver jumped out and laughed. He wore a wifebeater that failed to hide the clumps of hair emerging from his shoulders and back. The grease on his face added to the four-day growth of beard. "You're fucked," he said by way of greeting.

Two hours later, the mechanic at the garage studied the damage and announced, "Maybe you want to think about a new car. I'll give you an estimate tomorrow, but this baby looks like it has some hard miles on it."

Hughes nodded in silent agreement and asked about a ride to Boston.

"I can get my kid to give you a lift, if I can find him. But he'll charge you big time."

The kid showed up an hour later. He was skinny with a purple-dyed mohawk and a tee shirt that said, "Death is the best vacation." He was driving a small Japanese car of unrecognizable make with tailpipes so loud that they rattled adjacent windows. When he heard what Hughes wanted, he said, "A hundred bucks," scratched his stomach, took a step back, and waited.

Hughes glared at him and nodded. He climbed into the annoying vehicle and determined he only could make the trip by saying nothing to the kid. It was midnight when he finally got to the base of the hill and trudged up Beacon Street to Joy Street and his apartment. He thought to himself, *Maybe I should find another job.* Then he thought about the British racing green Mustang convertible with tan interior he had looked at two weeks ago and smiled to himself.

Chapter 3

A stream of August tropical air, heavy with moisture, blanketed the city. The sunshine was broken frequently with clouds thick as billowing trash bags, and dense rain would unexpectedly drench pedestrians caught unaware. The city seemed to shimmy at times.

The Miata was a sad case. Not only did Hughes lose the subject, missing out on at least a three-hundred-dollar fee, but the towing also cost three hundred dollars. The exorbitant cost of repairing the car sealed its demise. After some soul-searching, Hughes decided to go ahead and buy the Mustang GT convertible. The negotiations for purchase lasted fifteen minutes, then he piloted his new ride up to the valet at Mistral as an angry sun sunk low. The sweet feeling of success.

The bar inside was occupied by one middle-aged man, apparently a stockbroker, hungrily grinning at two female patrons, early entrants of the evening's games.

Angie, alone on bar duty at this time, was at the far service end chatting with a waiter of questionable gender. Hughes took a seat on the barstool nearest to the street-side corner and waited for her to notice him. He decided she was a perfect fit for the chic bar—as well as the new Mustang.

Angie moved with grace—the result of six years of modern dance she took years back. He decided her shoulders were a little strong for her body but figured necessary to support her impressive rack. Her hair cascaded over her shoulders like black velvet. Watching her from this angle, Hughes decided her butt was her best feature. He would have to pay more attention to her.

After a minute, she turned to check for any new customers, saw Hughes, and smiled. She walked over to him with a slight exaggeration of her hips, for which Hughes was grateful.

"Hi, big spender," she said. "What can I do to you?"

"Well, I was going to have a glass of wine, but the incredible selling techniques of the bartender have changed my mind. Do you have Black Bush?"

Angie gave one of her devastating smiles and said, "I'm sure. On the rocks?"

"Neat with a side of water."

She held the smile and moved off, returning with the Irish whiskey in a crystal-looking glass with water on the side. She placed the glasses on a cocktail napkin and said to him, "So, how's the new set of wheels?"

"Sweet. I love it. I can finally fit in the driver's seat. Want to go for a ride?"

"Anytime. But I'll have to get a nifty hat if you are riding around with the top down."

"I take a top down every chance I get."

"Don't I know it."

Hughes took a small sip of his whiskey and savored it.

People started to filter in and Angie kept a close eye on newcomers.

"Getting busy," she said. "After-work crowd—those who are working. Most of the city's away."

Two guys in short sleeves took barstools three down the bar. Angie smiled at them. "Be right with you," she said.

"What time are you wrapping up here? Time for a bite to eat later?"

"I won't be out of here until after midnight. Meet you back at the apartment."

He smiled. "Yours or mine?"

"Don't you love this double rent?" she said with just a hint of sarcasm. "I'll swing by your place, but it'll be late."

She moved down the bar to her customers with another slight swing to her hips that was not lost on Hughes. He sat and people-watched. Many of the women wore clingy summer dresses that kept his interest. After a couple of minutes of serving tall glasses of wine and drinks with limes, Angie strolled back. "Something to eat while you're here?"

"Sure, bring me the tuna tartare and a margherita pizza when you have a chance."

The tuna tartare was always mind-boggling delicious, and the pizza was better than ninety percent of the pizza parlors he's been in. The food came along at a leisurely pace and Hughes relaxed. Angie stopped back when she had a chance to chat. With the Mustang convertible parked outside and Angie smiling at him, he felt the good life.

He dawdled and watched the scene for an hour and a half, then got bored, waved to Angie, and had the valet bring the Mustang around. The summer night was warm with a tropical feeling, glazed with city grit.

Hughes knew the valets, having done some work for Mistral in the past making sure the fees for parking were turned in properly, and chatted briefly with them. He watched as a Ferrari and an outrageous Audi sports car pulled up but thought the Mustang held its own as he fired it up and listened to the twin pipes rumble with power.

He left the top down as he drove slowly the couple of minutes to Beacon Hill, where he found a spot on Chestnut Street, only a block away from his apartment.

Trees on the street were heavily leaved, and the air was musty and perfumed from the window boxes on the townhouses. He made his way up the steep street and around the corner to Joy Street. He paused and looked around at the front entrance to his building out of habit. Bumper-to-bumper cars parked on the street. A soft woman's laugh from below on Boston Common. Otherwise, it was quiet except for the white background noise of the city.

He climbed the stairs to his apartment, let himself in, and dropped his linen jacket on the back of a chair. He went for a beer from the refrigerator, then thought better of it, and pulled out a bottle of spring water.

He lay down on the couch and tried to watch the late news on television, but it bored him. His mind drifted and he found himself thinking unclean thoughts about Angie. A light sleep came with it. He woke with a start, hearing scratching at the door. He started to sit up as Angie came in, tired from the long bartender shift.

"Hi, peaches," she said. "Where are the candles and wine?"

He grinned at her. "All gone. The Linguini twins came over, drank the wine, and exhausted me."

Angie smiled. "Works for me. I'm pooped too. Maybe I can get right to sleep."

"Fat chance. You're looking way too good."

"Even with everything sagging? It was a busy night. I thought everyone was out of town in the hot summer. Got something cold and nonalcoholic?"

"Believe it or not, I think I have a bottle of ice tea in the fridge."

"That would be perfect." She plopped down on the couch, spread her legs out, and unbuttoned the top button on her white blouse. Even as a tired bartender, she looked great, Hughes thought. He broke out some ice from a tray, filled a glass with the ice tea, and brought it to her. She smiled up at him with large, appreciative hazel eyes as she took the glass and a deep sip.

Angie pulled her legs up onto the couch and yawned. "I'm really exhausted. It's beddy-bye time." She got up, stretched, and started for the bedroom, slipping out of her blouse and skirt on the way. Hughes watched her go with a goofy smile on his face, then followed her.

They both slept until the crashing of garbage cans outside woke them up. Angie pulled herself out of bed and tiptoed nude to the kitchen. Hughes rolled over and pulled the covers up. He knew he had much to do, but in a sleepy haze, couldn't quite remember what. Finally, the smell of fresh coffee got him out of bed. He met Angie in the kitchen, put his arms around her for a morning hug, feeling her silky warmth.

"Easy, big fella," she said, slipping out of his grasp. "I need a shower and have much to do today. No time to play."

"You sure?" he said. "After all, you were talking about my big fella."

She grinned at him. "Both big fellas have to settle down. I've got places to go, things to do."

He backed off. "Working tonight?"

She poured two cups of coffee, handing one to Hughes with a smile. "Off tonight. Have to pull a double tomorrow. Today is a day to get caught up on errands."

"How about we meet for cocktails and dinner later?"

"Sounds good to me. I should have everything wrapped up around five. I've got to do some shopping. Lord & Taylor's having a sale, so I thought I would try to pick something up so I stop looking like someone from Dracula's castle."

Hughes sipped his coffee. It was surprisingly good. He could never figure out how Angie's coffee was better than his. "OK, how about our standby, Abe & Louie's? I'll meet you at the bar at five-thirty. Work for you?"

She sauntered back into the bedroom, searching for her bra and panties. "Perfect," she called out to him. "I won't be late. There are more cougars there than in the Rockies."

Hughes smiled. He also started looking for clothes.

Chapter 4

The brownstone wore its elegance like an Armani tuxedo. In fact, much of Marlboro Street seemed to have a lock on charm. Even the tiny plots in front of the buildings were perfectly flowered and trimmed. Hughes thought he would have trouble affording some of the door knockers.

The heavy lion's head knocker he confronted at number seventy-four was no exception. After the first two heavy thumps, the door swung open. A stocky, bald man who was about seventy-five and wearing a faded suit and horn-rimmed glasses so thick it made his eyes look larger than they were stood at the door and smiled.

"You must be that private detective. I'm Ira Levine. It was my wife, Sara, who called you. Glad to meet you," he said. "Come in. Come in. Would you like to see my glass cane collection?"

"Glass canes? That sounds a little risky." Hughes entered slowly, looking around at the cluttered and dark front room. Windows to the street were heavily curtained and opaque. There was elaborate crown molding rimming the high ceiling, and the floor was well past any sheen.

It smelled vaguely like a nursing home and contrasted sharply with the soft warmth outside.

Ira shuffled deep into the room, stopping at the far wall. He pointed up and said, "Look at those. The largest collection of glass canes in North America, although some of the European collectors beat me by a mile."

Hughes looked up at the wall. Neatly arranged in rows were about twenty glass walking sticks, some with intricate swirls spun through them, others with etched sides and elaborate handles. None of them looked very sturdy. He didn't know what to make of them.

"That's very impressive. I've never seen any like those before," Hughes said. Then he noticed the glass jars scattered around the perimeter of the room and filled with what appeared to be marbles. Hughes saw several of these jars, each about a foot high, crammed with multicolored balls.

Noticing the stare, Ira said, "Oh, yes, I also have the largest marble collection in North America. And maybe everywhere," he added with more than a hint of pride. Hughes stared. Ira smiled broadly.

"Come, come with me upstairs to meet Sara," Ira muttered and led him to a wide stairway, shuffling along like someone wearing furry bedroom slippers. Hughes felt the pit in his stomach growing like warm yeast. The stairway heralded back to the Gilded Age, with walnut wainscoting and a railing polished from years of use following the stairs upward.

Climbing steeply upward, Hughes was led into a somewhat brighter room decorated in what only could be called Brooklyn Baroque. Inside, he saw a soft-looking, pear-shaped woman wearing a muumuu that fluttered around her like a loose tent in the wind. Her mousy-brown hair was pulled into a bun at the back of her head. She looked like someone you never wanted to stand behind in line at the Registry of Motor Vehicles.

"Find our son fast and bring him back," she snapped without introduction.

Hughes never turned down a client, but he was regretting answering this call. He paused, then summoning his best commanding voice, said, "How can I help?"

Sara was eyeing him like something on the bottom of her shoe.

Ira jumped in. "Now, Sara, let Mr. Hughes introduce himself and sit down. May I get him some coffee or tea?" He fidgeted in his chair.

"Good idea. I need to see what this guy is made of." She pointed to a worn wingback chair. Hughes sat down. She continued to eye him suspiciously.

Hughes gave her a smile. It was time to bring out his charming persona. He sat straight up and said, "Mrs. Levine, I've been in business for some time. I handle all types of cases, mostly criminal cases for corporations, such as theft, embezzlement, substance abuse, and so forth. I can probably help you, or I can recommend someone else who can." He paused to let her think.

Sara said nothing for a minute or two. As she studied Hughes, Ira shuffled in precariously handling a tray, upon which were perched mismatched cups and a small pitcher of coffee. He managed to get the tray down on the coffee table and grinned at his wife.

"How do you take your coffee, Mr. Hughes?"

"Black, thank you," Hughes replied and sat back. Sara continued to stare at him.

The room had an antique feel to it, with dust as heavy

as gravy in some corners. Hughes spotted a couple more glass jars filled with colorful marbles. He waited to hear the story, knowing immediately it would come from Sara, even though Ira would be more reasonable.

Sara started in. "Nineteen years ago, my father asked us to adopt a son. He was in New York Hospital. We didn't know who the parents were, but my father was adamant. We were childless, so we did the adoption." She paused and analyzed Hughes's expression. He made sure his face was as blank as an empty page. The harsh rasp of a motorcycle outside rattled through the townhouse like a distant omen of dread.

After a minute, when Hughes said nothing, she continued. "We raised Arnold like he was our own. There were some problems. He ran away from boarding school a couple of times, had some issues with venereal diseases and drugs. But we had high hopes for him. Now he's missing and my father, who is very ill, is considering cutting us out of his will to reflect what he considers our negligence."

Hughes took a sip of his coffee. Ira sat across the room, looking expectantly. Finally, Hughes said, "So are you asking me to find Arnold?"

"Exactly. You must find him and bring him back to us, so we can show that we are responsible parents," Sara said.

Hughes thought for a minute. "What is the relationship of Arnold to your father?" he asked.

"That is none of your concern," she said curtly. "What we need to know is when will you do this and how much will it cost?"

"Both of those things depend on where Arnold is, why he took off, and if he will cooperate. At his age, he is entitled to be where he wants to be."

Ira spoke up for the first time with a slight quiver in his voice. "We are afraid Arnold may be using drugs and mixed up with some bad people."

"Never mind that," Sara cut in sharply. "Mr. Hughes doesn't need to hear any unproven speculation."

It was clear to Hughes she did not want him to know everything about Arnold's disappearance, so he'd be going in pretty much blind. He was quiet for a minute. Aside from a couple of bar audits, business was flat, and a fat client should not be thrown away. Ira and Sara, despite the poor housekeeping and strange hobbies, looked like they could afford big checks.

Finally, he said, "My fee will be $500 a day for full-time work, prorated back accordingly if less than a full day, plus actual expenses. I can start tomorrow and see what I can do. I will report daily as to my progress."

Ira and Sara looked at each other. Ira shrugged. Sara turned to Hughes and nodded. He took that as an acceptance and said, "I'll send you a confirming letter as to my protocol and fees. But I need as much information as you have. Where do you think Arnold is?" He took a small sip of coffee, placed the cup down, and waited.

Sara sprung from her chair and went to a small walnut desk in the corner of the room. Opening the top drawer, she pulled out a tan file folder. She handed it to Hughes and plopped back into her chair. He opened it and sifted through some credit card statements and handwritten notes until he found a picture of an older boy with frizzy, reddish hair and a soft, bloated face sitting morosely at a table at some kind of family function.

"We think he went to New Jersey," Sara said. "We don't know much about New Jersey except that it's close to New York. We think he knows someone there."

"New Jersey's fairly large," Hughes said, scanning through the folder. "Any idea where in Jersey?" From the bank and credit card statements, he saw some ATM withdrawals and transactions from gas stations in Sea Bright and Asbury Park. "Does Arnold have a car?"

Sara looked at her husband, who looked back blankly. Finally, she said, "He took off with our Mercedes-Benz. It's a gray sedan. A nice car."

"Do you have a plate number?"

Ira shrugged and looked over at Sara, who continued to look at Hughes like he was an annoying salesman. "I don't know it," he said. "Do you, Sara?"

"Of course not. But it has Massachusetts plates on it. How many Mercedes-Benz cars from Massachusetts can there be in New Jersey?" she said with a bit of scorn in her voice.

The room went quiet for a moment. Hughes looked at Sara, then Ira. He stifled a smile. "OK, I will take this on. I'll do some Internet searches from the financial statements you gave me and do some telephone work. Then I'll head down to the Jersey Shore and see if I can find Arnold. Nothing guaranteed. The hardest thing to do is find someone who does not want to be found."

Ira took a tentative step forward. "Mr. Hughes, this is very important to us. Please find Arnold and bring him back. If only so we can talk to him," he said.

"Let me study what you gave me. I'll contact you tomorrow once I put together a game plan."

With that, Sara turned and wandered out the room without a further word.

Ira looked worried, then said, "I'll show you out. And let me show you some of my marble collection."

He led Hughes to a corner of the dark and almost gothic

room and held up a large glass jar filled to the top with multicolored glass orbs.

Then glancing to the stairs, Ira said, "Let's step outside, Mr. Hughes. You should know a little about Arnold."

They went out the front door to the short front walkway. Traffic on Storrow Drive could be heard in the distance like a vibrating hum. The sweet smell of tended flowers filled the air. Ira turned to Hughes and started talking in an almost whisper.

"Sara's father was a chemist and made several discoveries that made him a lot of money. But he is a stern and angry man," Ira said. "Then one night, we got a call from him demanding we go to New York Hospital and make arrangements to adopt a particular baby."

"I guess that would be Arnold," Hughes mused.

"Yes. He never said where the baby came from." Ira paused. "Ivan — that's his name — had a longtime lady assistant. Very close. Maybe Arnold was the result of that relationship. She left right after we adopted Arnold. Another possibility is Arnold is from Sara's brother."

"Where's the brother now?"

"Passed a long time ago. He had muscular dystrophy and was confined to a wheelchair. The rumor was that Ivan would bring in prostitutes to service him. Arnold may be the result of one of those liaisons. In any case, it was a bad start."

"So Arnold is of questionable origin and that has stayed with him as he grew up?"

"I'm afraid so. But we raised him as our own and he is ours. He has never seemed happy. But we want him back to help him be a good person."

Hughes looked up the leafy and picturesque street.

After a minute, he said, "I'll do my best. Arnold's start is not his fault. Lucky, he has you and Sara."

"Thank you," Ira said softly and turned back into the townhouse.

Hughes stood for a minute thinking about the secrets hidden behind the painted and polished doors of the expensive homes. He walked away, looking at each.

Chapter 5

Walking into the cool of Abe & Louie's from the summer sidewalk outside was like plunging into a spring-fed lake.

Mario, the maître d', gave him a grin as he walked into the tiny entranceway. "Hey, Danny. Still chasing bad guys?"

Hughes had a case for the restaurant a couple of months back catching a cook and a dishwasher walking out the back door with a case of lobsters. After the fact, Mario said he had suspected the two perps, but Hughes discovered otherwise.

"Private eyes never sleep," Hughes replied. "I'm heading to the bar, but when I get lucky, how about a table for two outside for about 6:30?"

"I got you down," Mario said, sweeping his arm toward the bar.

The bar was already busy, mostly with the after-work guys in summer suits. It was apparent that an active summer evening was getting started. Mike, a bartender who was built like a cement truck, moved his bulk toward an empty stool and gestured for Hughes to sit, then gave him a high five by way of greeting. "What's your pleasure this evening?" he asked.

"How about a Ketel One martini on the rocks with a twist?"

Mike smiled. "Shaken, not stirred?" he asked.

Hughes smiled back. "You know best."

Mike served up an enormous chilled rocks glass. Hughes took a small sip and felt the icy drink give him a slight chill. Perfect.

The bar was filling up quickly as the scene changed from after-work to serious hilarity. A blonde, probably pushing forty, sat next to Hughes and gave him a smile. Mike noticed her immediately and greeted her by name. "Jenny, a cosmo?" he asked, and she nodded. She fiddled with her purse as Mike prepared and served the drink. As he placed the martini glass dripping with summer perspiration on the bar, she turned to Hughes and said, "Getting hot, isn't it?"

He got the double entendre and smiled back at her. "Seems like that's a constant problem for me."

She laughed as she took a sip from her stemmed glass. Hughes took a larger one from his rocks glass. He felt the vibe from her and wondered.

Glancing around the room, he noticed at least three faces he knew. *Bad spot, bad idea*, he thought, especially when Angie was meeting him. He purposely looked back at Mike and asked, "Good summer?"

Mike looked around, then at Jenny, and shrugged. "Goes by too fast," he replied, then leaned into the bar, blocking Jenny as effectively as a Patriots offensive guard. She had no choice but to look forward as Angie made her way through the crowd, now two deep at the bar. She was wearing black stretch tights under a long, stark-white blouse that ran to her thighs. Her silver hoop earrings amplified her jet-black hair. She had her heavy horn-rimmed glasses on. Hughes thought it was like having two girlfriends—one with a hint of Vegas, the other working in academia.

"Hi handsome," she said as Hughes got up and she slid delicately onto his barstool. Jenny turned the other way and surveyed the bar in full predatory mode.

Hughes looked appreciatively at Angie. Suddenly, Jenny seemed second-rate, and he wondered again why he even considered wandering. "Hi, babes," he said. "Get everything done?"

"Yes, thank God. Summer shopping is definitely different. The sales help seem to be dreaming about beaches instead of assisting customers." She smiled at Mike, who slid over like a gravel truck. "How about an ice-cold chardonnay?" she asked.

"You bet, beautiful," he replied and placed down a paper cocktail napkin in front of her on the bar. A perfectly poured glass of wine arrived in seconds.

Hughes had to stand just behind her, and the decibel level began growing in direct proportion to the size of the crowd. Hughes glanced over and saw Jenny in a heated conversation with a guy who looked like an insurance salesman. He noticed her skirt had slid up to mid-thigh.

"So," Angie asked, stealing back his attention, "what's new in the world of private detectives?"

"Well, I took on a case, I think—still not sure about it—from an odd couple who lives on Marlboro Street," he said.

"What kind of case?"

"They have an adopted son who's run off. They want

me to find him and bring him back. It's going to pay well. Needed it."

"Where did he run off to? Going to be hard to find?"

"Looks like he's in New Jersey. On the Shore," Hughes replied. "I'll be heading there tomorrow."

"Oh, boy. I love the Jersey Shore. Great beaches. Room for a sidekick?" Angie asked before taking a tiny sip of her wine. She was the original cheap date.

His own martini was gone and Hughes signaled for a refill. He thought for a minute. He always worked alone, but maybe this could be a small paid vacation.

"Maybe after I get started. I need to get a feel for the layout there and where to look. If I can be a good sleuth, maybe you can join me; we can spend some summertime fun there." He saw Mario signaling him from the entrance and said to Angie, "Let's go for dinner. I'll take your wine."

Hughes carried Angie's glass and his second martini out to the sidewalk café, leaving Mike a sizable tip.

Mario seated them at a table with an almost blindingly white linen tablecloth along the rail next to the sidewalk. The air was cooling slightly, but a tropical-type haze hugged the city. Doormen at the Mandarin Oriental hotel across the street were shuffling expensive cars to the entrance, then away to wherever they parked them. In front of Abe & Louie's, the valets always left the more exotic cars at the curb to show them off. Tended to draw more women to the restaurant. Angie was still working on her first glass of wine when Hughes was ready for a third martini and ordered one when the pretty blonde waitress approached.

Angie looked at him. "Remember, martinis are like breasts: one is not enough and three is too many."

Hughes grinned. "You're right. This is my last for

tonight. It's just a beautiful evening; I want to feel mellow." Angie lifted her glass to him in mock salute.

Streetlights came on around eight o'clock, glowing orange in the hot evening. Hughes ordered a sirloin with a side of creamed spinach, while Angie was content with her Caesar salad with shrimp. Halfway through the meal, Angie ordered another glass of wine, while Hughes stuck to his promise and ordered a club soda. The food was superb, the night filled with promise and beauty. The Mustang was still at the curb three hours later, and they cruised it back to Beacon Hill slowly with the top down. Perfect.

When they got to the apartment, Hughes searched for a bottle of wine and found a sauvignon blanc in the fridge. Angie turned off the lights in the bedroom, letting the streetlight stream in through the large windows, softly bathing the room. Hughes uncorked the wine, poured two glasses, and went to find her in the bedroom. She was facing the bed with her back turned toward him. Her tights and blouse were next to her on the floor.

He watched her as she reached behind and unclasped her bra. She let it fall to the floor and he could see the side of her heavy breasts. She then pulled down her thong and tossed it aside. Shaped by her dance years, her bottom was round and high. A tiny tuft of black hair could be seen between her legs.

Hughes put the two glasses down, strode over to her, and put his arms around her, drawing her in close. She turned and stepped back, smiling. Her large nipples were dark rouge and fully erect. Below the slight curve of her belly, a thick triangle of black hair surrounded a thin slit. He could feel the warmth in his thighs and his heart rate accelerating. As always, it felt like first-time discovery.

* * *

Chirping outside woke him. He felt very refreshed and swung his legs easily out of bed. Angie lay on her side, breathing deeply, her jet-black hair framing her face like a halo. Walking softly in order to let Angie sleep in, Hughes got up and sat at his desk. He opened the "Arnold Levine" folder and began studying his notes.

It looked like Arnold went straight to the Jersey Shore. From the credit card statements, it seemed the first time he fueled up was on the Garden State Parkway. There were several food purchases, mostly in middle-range restaurants, Olive Garden, and McDonald's. There was an unusually large charge: four hundred and forty dollars at a place called Hitters Beach Club in Asbury Park.

Hughes thought about this for a minute. Hitters Beach Club did not sound like a strip club where Arnold could get ripped off with phony champagne, and it would be hard for him to spend that kind of money himself. Might be a good starting point. He studied the notes from the Levines and thought some more.

He was on his second cup of coffee when Angie rolled out of the bedroom, stretching like a feline. "Morning, tiger," she said as Hughes got up and handed her a cup of coffee.

"Morning. You slept like you were dead," he said.

"Pooped. Shopping is hard work. Fortunately, female genes prepare us for the onslaught. Ready for your big trip to the Jersey Shore today?"

"Yes, just have to get my gear together."

"How long do you think you'll be there?" Angie was rummaging around in the refrigerator looking for some fruit or anything for breakfast. "You really should make a trip to Whole Foods someday. This looks like Mother Hubbard's cupboard."

"Let's go out for a bagel down at Bruegger's. I'll buy." Hughes smiled.

"Hey, big spender, I'm on." Angie headed back into the bedroom and found a pair of jeans on the floor that she pulled on. Fit like a glove. "Any chance for me to join up with you in Jersey? I would love to hang out on the beaches for a couple of days."

"Maybe. I'll see how it goes. I'm vague on just how I'm going to find this guy." Hughes got out an extra-large black tee shirt and black jeans. He slipped on a pair of New Balance running shoes and watched Angie turn her back to him to pull on a bra.

"You know, you really don't need one of those things," he said.

"I don't want them to hang down to my knees later on. Support is good," she replied as she turned around and put on a white shirt. Hughes could only gawk and admire.

They walked the short distance over to Beacon Hill, then down to Bruegger's Bagels on Milk Street. The usual office workers rush was going on, and Hughes and Angie had to stand in line for five minutes. You could feel the stress in the air. Angie got her usual sesame with fat-free cream cheese, while Hughes opted for a garlic with a slice of onion and cream cheese.

Angie shook her head. "Looks like you're going to defeat the bad guy with your breath," she said, laughing.

"Nature's perfect food," he replied as they headed for a window table. Outside the day was steaming up and was threatening to be sweltering. They ate quietly for a minute, then Angie said, "Is what you're working on today dangerous?"

"The clients are strange and provided scant information. They want me to find and scoop up a son without telling me why he ran or what he may be into," Hughes said, then watched as a young guy in a seersucker suit did a double take on Angie to check her out.

Hughes smiled. "I'll head down and see where I'm going with it. Maybe if I get lucky, you can shoot down and we'll lay on the beach for a couple of days."

"Change of place, change of scene. I could use that," she said.

After breakfast, they walked slowly back up and over the hill to Joy Street. Once they were at the top, the Boston Common spread out below them like a green shag rug. It was already populated with people lying in small groups, savoring the summer morning. They were quiet. After some minutes, Angie asked, "Are you happy?"

Hughes shrugged.

"I mean in what you do. Are you happy being a PI?"

Hughes thought for a minute as they descended the hill and started coming up to his apartment. "I don't make enough money," he said.

"I don't think money is that important if you're happy with what you're doing," she said.

Hughes stopped and stared out across the Public Garden toward the high-rises shimmering in the growing heat. "I love it. I have adventures that I don't think many guys ever get. And what people do never ceases to amaze me. Yeah, I guess I'm happy. Especially, it seems, when I'm with you."

She reached out and took his hand and held it until they walked up the stairs.

Once back in his apartment, Hughes started packing. Into a leather duffel, he stuffed shorts and summer shirts along with solid shoes with rubber soles and toiletries. The Airweight .38 with the small belt holster went in on the bottom of the bag. He decided he was all set and ready to go and came to say goodbye to Angie.

"Heading out?" she asked.

"Yeah, if I leave now, I figure I'll be at the Jersey Shore sometime in the middle of the afternoon."

"Where are you staying?" she asked.

"Don't know yet. I'm going to Asbury Park to look around. Hopefully, I'll find a Holiday Inn or something. I'll call when I find something and let you know." He slung the bag over his shoulder, picked up his briefcase, and looked around the apartment. Angie turned and came to give him a minor kiss. It felt like a butterfly touch.

"Be careful," she said, turning away.

"Not to worry. Maybe you can swing down and guard me if this thing lingers on," he said.

"Say the word." She turned back to him again. Her smile was weak.

"See, ya, babe. Love ya," he said as he headed out the door. Angie closed it quietly behind him.

The car was resting under a large maple tree that already had dropped a few leaves onto the top. Hughes slung his bag into the trunk, put the briefcase in the back seat, and started the car, listening for a minute to its satisfying rumble. Then shifting into first, he pulled out and up Chestnut Street to Joy and around to Beacon Street. He picked up the Southeast Expressway five minutes later and headed south, settling into an easy sixty-five-miles-per-hour pace. He decided to take the Tappan Zee, then pick up the Garden State to the Jersey Shore. He felt comfortable and relaxed. As he drove west on the Mass Pike, green fields overgrown in the August sun slid by in a blur. Connecticut was lush with tinges of brown already as he picked up the Merritt Parkway.

As he cruised past SUVs laden with vacation gear, he reviewed the case in his head. Find Arnold and convince him to come home. Don't know which part of that will be the hardest. The kid's nineteen, so the beaches and clubs are the first places to look. The photo he had in his briefcase showed an awkward-looking guy with a soft face and tight, curly, red hair. Not a hunk. May be tough to sort him out from all the others littering the Jersey Shore.

After crossing the Hudson, he picked up the Garden State, initially facing tolerable traffic. There seemed to be an excessive quantity of Mercedes and BMWs on the road, reflecting the affluence spilling over from New York City. Thinking about Angie, especially her night moves, Hughes decided there was no really good reason why she could not join up with him, especially if the case was going to take a week or so.

Years ago, he attended a wedding in Red Bank. The wedding was not memorable, but where he stayed was. The Molly Pitcher Inn would be a nice place for a romantic interlude with Angie. Good food, a nice bar, and especially comfy beds. He headed for there.

Chapter 6

The night before, while Hughes and Angie had drifted into contented sleep in the Beacon Hill apartment, things were kick-starting in Asbury Park. A sultry and salty breeze whispered in from the sea. At the Wonder Bar, the strings of garish outside lights gave it a carnival atmosphere. It was alive and sad at the same time. A few afternoon partiers who had been overserved still were lingering in the outside table area.

Inside, Arnold Levine stood adjacent the sopping-wet, vinyl-topped bar. It was only half-occupied, but a steady stream of rock lovers and searchers was coming in and filling in the space.

Arnold was tall and very thin, his reddish, curly hair grown out almost to a dreadlock look. A soiled tee shirt that said "Knicks" hung on his frame, and the shorts he wore had a back pocket torn off. The flip-flops he was wearing failed to hide the grit on his feet. He was slightly swaying, like a wheat stalk in a light summer breeze.

On his right stood Bobby Musa, thickly muscled from hours of lifting heavyweights at the gym. The three top buttons of his black silk shirt were open, showing a heavy gold necklace. He wore his usual smug half-smile. He somehow looked older than his twenty-nine years. Musa pulled over a wooden barstool and pushed it toward Arnold so he could sit. Arnold glanced back at him with glassy-eyed gratitude.

"Karen," Musa called to the worn, blonde bartender, "two shots of Patron Silver." He placed a fifty on the bar, which Karen picked up with sullen indifference. He turned to Arnold.

"Arnie, baby, here's to making money and living well." He pushed one of the shots to Arnold and held his up in a toast. Arnold grimaced as they tossed down the tequila. Musa grinned at him, a predatory smile.

The bar was filling up and a ragged punk band was drifting onto the low stage, getting ready to warm up. The beach feel was unmistakable.

A group of the regular guys drifted in and gave a greeting to Musa. They checked out Arnold. Then Tony, an enormous, dark-skinned man with a shaved head and Popeye arms, spoke. "We're starting to worry about you. Looks like you are spending a lot of time with your bitch," he said, nodding toward Arnold. Arnold was staring at Karen, who was bending over arranging bottles under the bar, and didn't hear.

Musa laughed and said, "You have no idea. Eat your fuckin' heart out."

The guys chuckled and moved on.

He then felt a soft hand on his bottom and turned to his right to find Tiffany leaning across the bright-red bar, a low-cut tank top showing off expansive cleavage. She signaled to Karen for a Patron shot for herself.

"Hi, baby," Musa said. "Bout time. I didn't know how long I could be drinking with just me and Arnie."

Tiffany looked over at Arnold, who rewarded her with a lopsided grin.

Musa turned to Arnold. "Hang here for a minute. Me and Tiff have some business to discuss." He nodded to her and indicated the door to the outside patio area. She threw back the shot of tequila and headed outside with him.

Settling in on a corner picnic table, she said to him, "Bobby, why are you fucking around with that kid loser? I think we have better things to do. Margie said some of the group is heading down to AC to party. We're all staying in a suite at the Nugget. No way you can bring him."

"Baby, that loser is the heir to serious money. If his old man happens to fall over dead, he gets about ten mil. You never know; accidents happen." He smiled. "He's so fuckin' hooked now that he'll do just about anything for a fix. Especially take care of Uncle Bobby. But right now, I need some of Tiffany. Baby, it seems like a year ago I felt your soft lips on my dick."

"It was last week, lover, and I've been waiting for your call ever since. I had to come to the Wonder to find you."

"Well, you found me and I found you. Who's home at your place?"

"Doesn't matter. Let's go. But you can't bring that kid."

"He's wasted. I'll stick him back in the beach shack and we can head over to your place. But don't get pissed. I can only stay about an hour. I have a meeting with some heavies in Jersey City later."

"You won't believe what I can do in an hour."

They went back inside and found Arnold where they left him. As Musa went up to the bar, Karen signaled for him to come to the far corner. He left Tiffany trying to make small talk to Arnold. Musa followed Karen as she went to the other end of the bar.

She looked around, then said, "Bobby, you've got to get that kid out of here. I know he's underage and you get him totally shitfaced. Not good. We can both get in trouble."

"No problem, babe. We're gone."

"Don't bring him back."

Musa shrugged and headed back to Arnold and Tiffany. "Let's go. Come on, Arnie."

Arnold was quiet, then nodded. Musa helped him up from the barstool and the three of them headed out into the hot August night.

They deposited Arnold in a shack next to the beach, left him snoring on top of a stained bed, and headed to Tiffany's place in Musa's Camaro. She was living in an enormous antique house on a tree-lined street. It had fallen on hard times but still retained some old dignity. It was occupied by four other people, sometimes five, sometimes six. The lights were blazing on the ground floor, the rest of the house gloomily dark.

Walking in to the shambles of the living room, they were confronted with a male of undetermined age asleep on the couch. He was wearing only shorts and emitted an odor as strong as a horse stable. They walked past him and up the stairs to Tiffany's room. An hour later, Musa left the house, past the sleeping critter still on the couch, leaving Tiffany relaxing upstairs.

The Camaro started with strength and Musa headed north. He picked up the Turnpike and made his way to the Pulaski Skyway toward Jersey City. Off to the right, the landscape looked ugly and hostile. Pulling off near Sip Avenue into a gritty and harsh neighborhood, he found the Pit Bull Café next to a used tire garage. It was housed in a square cinder block building with peeling and faded white paint. The one window in front was small and high up, filled by a Miller beer sign lit in garish red neon. The front door was solid, painted a dull black.

Musa walked in and saw two men, both overweight, seated at the end of the bar and a table in the corner with two other men smoking cigars, watching a horse race on television. The bar smelled of stale beer, urine, and despair.

Adjusting to the dim light, Musa walked to the table and, receiving a nod from one of the men, sat down. Musa knew one. He was Freddy Barcinko, an older, heavy-shouldered man with a reddish pockmarked face and a tomato nose. The other man, younger and nervous, stared at Musa with bored malice. Barcinko signaled to the bartender, who ambled over carrying an enormous gut over his belt. Barcinko spun his finger around, signaling another round for all, and the bartender returned in a minute with three tall glasses filled three-quarters with amber fluid.

Barcinko took a sip and said, "To what the fuck do we owe the honor of this visit?"

Musa glanced at the other man. Barcinko noticed and said, "You can talk here. Vinnie is like family."

"Hi Freddy," Musa said. "I have a situation that maybe we can all profit from." He took a sip from his glass and winced slightly. The other two men sat silently. "I came across a creepy loser. He's a runaway from Boston. Doesn't know shit and has got himself a nice and heavy habit."

"No doubt assisted by persons unknown," Barcinko mumbled.

Musa shrugged. "Here's the deal. His old man has got serious coin and, according to the kid, has set him up with a trust that he can draw on. He needs the old man's permission but supposedly can get a couple of hundred large."

"I gather you figure you can get your hands on this money?"

Musa smiled. "You bet. All I have to do is increase the monkey on the kid's back to a gorilla and he'll do anything I say to get more. He'll be my piggy bank."

"So?" Barcinko said, looking around the room, "how do I profit?"

"I need a secure source of high-grade H. The kid is into snow and shit, but I need to get him into my back pocket. I'll pay whatever is decent street and maybe agree to a monthly bonus if all goes well."

Barcinko looked at the other man. He was dressed in a black silk suit with a white silk shirt buttoned to his neck underneath. "What to think, Vinnie? Does this asshole make any sense to you?"

Vinnie took his cigar and crushed it out on the tabletop. "How long does he think Pappy up in Boston will sit around watching the money disappear? Sounds like a lot of bullshit to me."

The two men at the bar grunted and stood. The one at the end, short and fat, farted and they both laughed. Money was thrown on the bar, and they sauntered out, giving Barcinko a little wave as they passed by. Musa waited until they were gone before continuing. The bartender disappeared into a back room.

"The kid tells me he's adopted. Doesn't know from where. But the old man lives and dies with him and gives him everything he wants. Been sending money right along. I figure if the kid is seriously hooked on me, he'll do whatever I say."

Barcinko and Vinnie looked at each other. After a

minute, Barcinko said, "So what's in it for us? You have a pet money machine and we're sucking wind?"

"I'll pay top dollar for regular supply. And if this thing works out, I'll kick in a 10% bonus every month. I need to keep this loser hooked big time. Worth it to me."

Barcinko stared at him for a long minute. "If I didn't know your old man, I'd tell you to go fuck yourself. I can do anything you want. Question is, do I want? Tell you what; you go on retainer to me, 4K a month. You get a guaranteed pipeline. You need more, you pay more. You need less, it's still 4K." He waited.

Musa knew that if he couldn't come up with the four thousand a month, he'd be paying serious vig and would be seeing collection guys crawling up his ass. A risk. He thought about it for a minute.

"OK, but let's do the deal for six months. We can talk more then."

Musa was mentally tabulating if he could squeeze five or six a month out of the kid. After six months, the kid would be a vegetable and he wouldn't need that much to keep him paying out.

Barcinko studied him. "I'm a stand-up guy. You better the fuck be one, too. Pepper will come by with the first batch. Call here and just tell whoever answers where you will be if I'm looking for you. I expect the first four upon delivery."

Musa swallowed hard, then nodded. He stood up and held out his hand. The two men ignored him and turned to the television set in the corner. Musa walked out on legs as shaky as a 4.5 on the Richter. He got in his car and headed south. The first thing he planned to do when he got back to Asbury Park would be to check on wasted

Arnold to make sure he was not off base with the Jersey City boys.

Barcinko looked at Vinnie after he heard Musa's car roar out of the parking lot.

"What do you think about that clown?"

Vinnie took a gulp from his glass and slouched down. "His cousin is Patty Demarko from Elizabeth. Always been OK with us. Not made but close and has done some favors. I think we give the kid some space and see what he can do. What can it hurt? Obviously, he's got a stoned fish on the line. Who knows? Maybe money for nothing."

Barcinko nodded. He took his phone from his pocket and hit a speed-dial button. After a moment, he said into the phone, "Mikey, when you pick up the monthly from Stone Pony, ask Stanley if he knows Bobby Musa and what he thinks of him. I want to make sure he's not a snitch to anyone."

After a pause, he said, "If any questions, let me know right away. Maybe a small-time business partner."

There was a pause, then, "You got it."

He punched the call off and looked at Vinnie, who nodded and lifted his arm. "Get off your ass and bring us another round," he yelled to the bartender. "And turn the fuckin' volume up on the TV."

A faint animal smell surrounded both men as they stared up at the glowing panel on the wall.

Chapter 7

Traffic on the Garden State filled suddenly and then crawled at a turtle pace. Hughes didn't pull into the Molly Pitcher Inn until late afternoon. The sky was already turning into a ruddy glow. He pulled the Mustang into the circular front drive and stopped in front of the entrance. No one hustled out, so he stretched and popped the trunk, pulling out his bag and briefcase. He walked into the lobby and found a young woman at the desk. She was about twenty, very fit, healthy-looking, and had a tag on her formable front that said, "Ginger Christmas." She was wearing a white blouse, open at the neck. A thin gold necklace could be seen. She gave Hughes a perky smile and said, "Welcome to the Molly Pitcher."

Hughes smiled back and said, "Really?"

Confused, she replied, "What?"

"Ginger Christmas? Is that a real name?"

With a hint of a blush, she grinned and said, "Yep. I hear that a lot. But it's mine and I love it."

"Well, I love it, too."

Ginger Christmas discreetly looked Hughes up and down and moved her shoulders back slightly. It had the desired effect. "Um, do you have a reservation, sir?" The "sir" was drawn out.

Hughes felt that nice mutual chemistry feeling. Made him feel younger than his thirty-six years. "Yes, I called from my car about two hours ago."

She glanced out at the Mustang sitting in front and searched the screen sunk into the countertop. "Yes, sir. I see it. A standard with a king-size bed. But I can put you into a suite for the same price, if you like. Will you be alone?"

Some bad thoughts flowed through his head. Then he said, grinning, "Well, I'm alone now but not sure about later."

Ginger Christmas kept her head down, then looked up into his eyes and slid a key across the counter. Room 300, overlooking the river. Enjoy your stay, sir."

"Thank you, Ginger. I think I will."

Hughes found his way to the third floor and let himself into the suite. It was very nicely appointed. It had a large living room with a beige couch and an oval coffee table in front of it. Two side chairs with paisley seats and wooden arms were positioned at an angle on the other side of the coffee table. A desk and chair were in the corner. It smelled like freshly cut flowers. Dominating the room was a large window overlooking the river. Yellow sunlight poured into the room.

Looking out the window, Hughes remembered from the brochure that the river was called Navesink. It was wide at this end, flat and placid, not showing any current. It glistened in the waning sun. A small marina, crowded with bright-white boats, cluttered the left bank. Several boats were motoring up the river, leaving sparkling, long trails behind. Directly below, three floors down, was a large patio. A couple was sitting there opposite each other and leaning forward like they were whispering a secret. Hughes stood for a minute, taking it in, then whispered to himself, "I love my job."

The bedroom contained an enormous bed topped with more pillows than two people ever could use.

He found a suitcase stand in the closet, set it up to the side, and placed his bag on it. He moved back into the living room and opened his briefcase on the desk. He took out the .38, placed it into the drawer, and covered it with the brochures that were in there. He looked at his watch. Already pushing six o'clock.

Stiff from the drive, he stretched and plopped onto the bed, flicking on the television with the remote. Tuned to Fox News, he started to let the vibrations of the drive dissolve. Before he could relax, the phone rang. It was Ginger Christmas softly reminding him to move the Mustang.

After putting the car in a spot on the side and returning to the lobby, he went to the front desk and smiled. "I have a question. What are the hottest clubs on the Shore?" he asked Ms. Christmas.

She looked perplexed, and Hughes realized she was probably thinking he was asking her out.

Before she could answer, he said, "I have to find someone, and I think some of the clubs on the Shore will be a good place to start looking."

He couldn't tell if she was relieved or saddened.

She shrugged, then said, "The Stone Pony is famous. Springsteen got his start there. The Wonder Bar is close by. They're both in Asbury Park."

"Is Asbury Park the best place to look?"

She shrugged again. "The Shore is full of clubs. Asbury Park, Sea Girt, Sea Bright, Belmar. Good luck."

"What's the best?" he asked.

She thought for a minute, then said, "I don't go to many clubs, but I think The Stone Pony is the most famous. It's been around forever. Keeps getting closed up, then reopens. Maybe start there." She gave a wane smile.

Hughes glanced at his watch. Way too early to go to any bars or clubs. He decided to take a walk outside, find a place for dinner, and figure out a game plan.

"Thanks, Ginger," he said.

"You're welcome, sir," she replied. More of an invitation than a dismissal.

Chapter 8

The lights on the Garden State Parkway yellowed the night sky as Musa motored back to Asbury Park. He didn't see any cops, but occasionally the lights of a car he passed at high speed would flash at him, an irritated driver behind the wheel.

The town was empty and dark when he pulled onto the street two blocks from the beach. The faint sound of surf could be heard amid the stillness. The houses on Mason Street looked sinister and were sagging from the pummeling of the strong ocean winds over time. Several were boarded up but showed signs of entry by druggies and the homeless.

Musa could see a small group of young black men slouching under a weak streetlight two blocks away. He absently reached under the seat to touch the Glock he had stuffed there.

Number forty-two stood like a tired retiree, a soft glow showing through the downstairs window. Musa pulled into the dirt driveway on the side and silenced the car. He sat for a minute in the quiet, senses alert. Soundless. He pulled the Glock 16 out from under the seat and stuffed it underneath his belt. He stood up next to the car, listening and watching all around. Empty.

Walking to the front entrance, his footsteps sounding loud, he opened the door with a key and slid in. The glow was coming from a light over the stove in the kitchen in the back. As his eyes adjusted, he saw Arnold Levine in a modified fetal position on the frayed couch. He went to him and looked down. The stench coming off Arnold was like rotting roses. His stained tee shirt was pulled up and revealed his stomach, white as the belly of a fish. Ribs were showing through the thin skin.

Musa shook him. "Wake up, dude, time to rise and shine."

There was no response. For a minute, Musa was afraid Arnold was dead. Again, he shook him, more violently. A death rattle-type moan came from him, and his eyes suddenly popped open, unfocused, staring up at the ceiling. Musa let out a small sigh of relief.

He turned and went into the kitchen and found a tin of Maxwell House coffee in the back corner of the counter. He took it out and pulled the plastic cover off, sniffing the contents. Stale, finely ground coffee. He turned over the can and, using his fingernail, snapped off the seemingly attached metal bottom. From the false bottom, he took out a styrene bag containing an off-white powder. Using a spoon from the cabinet drawer, he cooked up a small quantity of the powder into a liquid.

Leaving it bubbling on a saucer, Musa went to the rusty electric toaster next to the coffee pot. He took off the crumb-catcher bottom and pulled out a hypodermic needle that was hidden there. He put the end of the needle into the liquid and pulled up the plunger. He held it up to the dim light, studied it, then turned and headed back to Arnold.

Chapter 9

H ughes put on fresh jeans, a white silk tee, his trusty navy blazer with the brass buttons, and his brand-new Allen Edmonds brown loafers. He walked out through the lobby and into the thick August dusk. He could smell cut grass. Across the street, a red sign over a thick wooden sculptured door advertised "Anthony's Ristorante." Down the street, he could see a couple of wooden frame houses and an empty lot covered in weeds. The restaurant looked inviting, and Hughes realized he had not eaten since he had left Boston.

Traffic was light as he crossed the street and made his way to it. Inside was dark and cool. A long mahogany bar was on the right; it was separated from the dining tables by a shoulder-high wall. A couple was seated in the far corner of the bar, chatting and smiling. Behind the bar, eyeing Hughes, was a tall woman. as his eyes adjusted to the dim lighting, he saw she had black hair cut into a short pageboy, had on minimal makeup, and was wearing a red blouse with the buttons straining against an impressive chest. Her eyes were an unusual blue, contrasting against the dark hair. There was the faintest hint of lipstick. She smiled at Hughes as he approached and slid onto a stool.

"Hi," he said, "where's Anthony?"

"No such person as Anthony," she said. "Unless you want to call Bernie, the owner, that but I wouldn't recommend it." Her voice was low and soft with a hint of humor behind it.

"I'm Dan Hughes," he said, sticking out his hand.

She shook it with a firm and dry grip. "Annie Treat."

Hughes smiled. "A. Treat? Appropriate."

She smiled back. "Having dinner?"

The menu was already on its way.

"Yep."

"Something to drink?"

"A Ketel One martini on the rocks with a twist." Opening the menu, he asked, "What's the best thing?"

She thought for a minute, then said, "The veal piccata is terrific."

"Thanks. A fairly famous restaurateur told me to always ask that. If the answer is everything, leave. I'll have that with a side of penne."

"I'm glad I passed the test," she said as she moved away to prepare the martini. Hughes could see she wore tight stretch pants, filled with the backside of an aerobics instructor.

She prepared the drink perfectly and served it on a cardboard coaster. With no other business, she paused and asked if it was OK.

Hughes took a sip and nodded. "Perfect."

He took another taste, then asked, "I need to find someone. I'm thinking the best place to look is in rock clubs. Are there any you would recommend? I was told the best ones are probably in Asbury Park. What do you think?"

"All the ones you find there are probably the most

sleazy, but the Jersey Shore is filled with clubs. Good luck. I hope you have a strong stomach," she said. "Let me put your food order in."

As she walked down the length of the bar, Hughes mentally removed her pants.

The veal piccata was indeed terrific. A few people drifted in, but the bar remained uncrowded, giving him an opportunity to chat with Annie.

"Who are you looking for? An old flame?" she asked.

"No, I'm a PI. I'm trying to locate a runaway."

"A PI? Like on TV?"

"Not exactly like TV. I hardly ever get beat up and, until tonight, hardly ever meet a beautiful woman."

She took the flirt in stride.

"I could use a guide. No strings attached."

She was silent for a minute. "I don't get off until eleven."

"That would work. Maybe show me a club nearby. We could have a drink, and you could introduce me to the Shore."

Annie smiled. "No strings and no expectations. I could use a drink after working here. There's a club in Sea Bright that I go to once in a while. The crowd is a little older, so it's a little more civilized. I could meet you here a little after eleven. But I won't stay late."

"Sounds good. What's its name?" Hughes asked, taking a sip of his second martini.

"Beachcomber. Meet me here and you can follow me there." She saw some customers at the end of the bar and walked away and waited on them without another word.

Hughes watched her for five or six more minutes, then drained the rest of his martini and replaced the glass on the bar. He waved to Annie and she smiled back. He thought, *I love my job.*

Hughes retrieved the Mustang from its spot in the back, put the top down, and rumbled out onto the street. It was still warm with a soft haze settling in. The moon hung full and important in the evening sky. Hughes inhaled and felt the air flow over and through the car. He headed south on Maple Avenue, admiring some of the classic frame houses still standing with dignity. Picking up Route 36, he turned east toward Long Branch and continued to the beach road. He turned left, following signs to Sea Bright. On the ocean side, dunes and breakwaters had been built up like prison walls, keeping out the storm surges.

Beach houses of assorted styles and sizes ran in a row on the left. Windows open to the breezes, beach towels draped over railings, and toys scattered in the sand paid homage to summer.

Hughes let the car amble slowly. He spotted the Beachcomber sitting in the sand, advertising a band called the Kitchen Sink. He decided to wait and let Annie show it to him.

He turned left onto Rumson Road and gawked at the mansions and estates, then made his way back to Red Bank. He still had a couple of hours until eleven o'clock and decided to return to the Molly Pitcher to organize his thoughts. He parked the Mustang, left the top down, and went through the lobby.

Ginger Christmas was gone, replaced by a smooth-faced young man. Hughes asked if coffee could be sent to his room. The front desk attendant, with the name badge "Randy," was eager to please and agreed to have a pot sent right up.

Back in the room, with the nighttime marine lights twinkling on the river outside as a backdrop, he sat at the desk and pulled out a legal pad, making notes to himself:

- Check clubs, transient housing, and hostels for signs of Arnold
- Get copies of his photo to show to bartenders, desk clerks, etc.
- Find the local paper and place an ad, "Seeking Arnold," with his cell number
- Keep calling his cell phone
- Call the clients to see if they have heard anything

Hughes leaned back and thought. If Arnold is at the Jersey Shore, he could be anywhere. *Where would a runaway, supposedly smart but a dumb kid, be? Libraries to use their computers? Maybe. Still think he would be looking to get laid. Check gay clubs as well.*

Hughes got up and went to the window. Lights in the marina lit up the docked and sleeping boats. A couple of the larger ones had lights glowing from inside, signaling occupants. Probably having romantic cocktails and enjoying being alive. He sipped some of the delivered coffee and decided this case might be tougher than he first thought.

Chapter 10

At ten-thirty, Hughes pulled on his loafers and blazer and made his way across the street to Anthony's. Tables were empty except for a serious couple huddled together in the far corner table and a couple at the bar, just leaving. Annie still looked fresh.

"Hi sleuth," she smiled.

Standing at the bar, Hughes smiled back. "I think a coffee, if still available. And maybe a Bushmills, neat, on the side."

"Coming right up," she said, moving off to get the coffee. Hughes studied her with close interest.

She came back within a minute with the coffee and free-poured two fingers of the Irish whiskey into a rocks glass. She looked at Hughes warily. "If we are going to a club, I will only stay a few minutes. Working again, the day shift."

"That's fine," Hughes replied. "I just need to get a feel for the culture to see if the search makes sense. No strings."

"OK, I'll take my car and you can follow me there. I have to close out. Pretty slow, so I'll start now. Sip your drink and I'll be ready to go in ten minutes."

Annie pulled the cash drawer and went in back. The

apparent manager dimmed the lights as a clue. He gave Hughes a look like he was a spider on his shoe.

When Annie came back to the bar, Hughes noted she was now wearing a beige tee with the same stretch pants. She did not look like she had just worked a full shift. "All set?" she said.

"Ready to go," Hughes replied, tipping the remainder of Bushmills into his coffee cup and drinking it down. He got up with mild anticipation and followed Annie out to the lot behind the restaurant. As she unlocked a white Prius, he told her he would get his Mustang and meet her in front of the Molly Pitcher. He strode across the street, got into his car, and pulled to the front of the inn, where he saw Annie's car.

Seeing him, she pulled out and started driving the same route he had taken earlier. As she drove expertly and quickly, he was reminded of what Ian Fleming once said: "Women who drive fast are usually beautiful and are always exciting." Annie fit both counts.

He followed along closely, again turning left on the beach road, then going almost to the end where the Beachcomber sat in the sand. Cars were strewn at different angles in the parking lot, and fire torches flamed around the outside bar. People were streaming in and out. Young women, in groups of three and four, stood around the beach bar, some wearing bikini tops. The band was milling around a small stage set in the sand to the side, apparently getting ready for another set. Hughes and Annie walked around, she nodding to a couple of people who obviously knew her.

"Come on," she said. "Let's look inside."

Hughes followed her without a word. Inside of the club, there was an unoccupied dance floor and a long bar along the far side. It was only three-quarters full, apparently because it was getting late.

"Come on," Hughes said. "I'll buy you a drink."

"Sure," she smiled.

The bartender, heavily built, balding, and with a paunch, came over and looked at them.

Annie ordered a gin and tonic, Hughes a Jameson on the rocks. As the bartender served the drinks, Hughes took out a photo of Arnold and showed it to the bartender. "Ever seen this guy?" he asked.

The bartender stared at the picture, then at Hughes. He shook his head and picked up the twenty Hughes had thrown onto the bar.

"OK," Hughes said as he watched the bartender toss the bill into a tip cup next to the register. The bartender then walked to the far end of the bar where three men in jeans and tee shirts were standing. Hughes saw him say something to them and nod toward him and Annie. The three men looked over.

Hughes felt an electric shock of adrenaline. Turning back to Annie, he said, "Well, this is the kind of place I think I should be looking, but I think I'd rather chat with you right now."

From the corner of his eye, he could see two of the three goons from the other end of the bar approaching them. He felt their menacing presence like a cold fog but ignored them.

One of them was Musa. His face was icy hard.

The other was Musa's friend, a tall and wiry guy with a thin goatee hiding an acne-pocked face. His lower lip hung like a soiled rag. He wore greasy hair slicked back. A chain hung off the belt of his dirty jeans.

Musa tapped Hughes hard on his shoulder. Hughes stopped talking but did not turn around.

Musa said in a low growl, "Not from around here." A statement, not a question.

Hughes turned, his eyes steeling like the marbles he saw in Ira Levine's jars. He leaned forward and stared into Musa's bottomless eyes. "Just visiting," he said slowly.

"Why are you asking stupid questions?" Musa stared back, his friend taking one step to the side.

"Mind your own business," Hughes said, gesturing to Annie to move away.

"Who the fuck do you think you're talking to? Know who I am? I'll ask you again, why the fuck you asking questions?"

Hughes sized up Musa. Heavier than he and with weight-lifting muscles. He glanced to his right to the friend and thought he was even more dangerous. "None of your business," he said, turning back to the bar.

Musa gave him a hard, open-hand slap to the back of his head and grabbed his shoulder, spinning him around. He saw Musa clench his fist and telegraph a punch to his face. Hughes's officer candidate hand-to-hand combat training instinctively kicked in, and he stomped his heel onto Musa's right foot. Musa lost his breath and bent forward. Hughes then head-butted him in the nose; immediately blood sprayed from his face and across the bar. The friend jumped back and took out a sap, swinging it at Hughes in a wide arc. At the last second, Hughes brought up his arm to protect his head and took the sap on his forearm. He felt his arm immediately go numb.

The friend reared back for another hit, but Annie picked up a bottle off the bar and hit him in the back of the head. Stunned for a minute, he turned to Annie and started for her. The bartender intervened, slamming the top of the bar with a baseball bat. Everyone froze. Annie pulled out her phone and hit the speed dial to 911. She screamed into the phone that murder was about to happen at the Beachcomber. Within seconds, the detail cop from the parking lot ran in.

Musa, holding his nose, turned and disappeared into the crowd. His friend followed. The cop, excited, looked at Hughes and Annie and said, "What the hell is going on?"

The bartender screamed, "These assholes started a fight. Lock them up."

The cop looked around, confused as to who was fighting whom. Hughes was holding his arm, which was totally numb. Somehow, he also got a long scratch on his right cheek that was oozing blood. Annie was standing to the side, pale as paper, and breathing heavily.

"Outside!" the cop said to Hughes and Annie while still looking around for the other combatants. They walked out onto the beach, the crowd already losing interest as they continued their mating dance.

Outside, they were taken to the side by the police officer. "IDs," he demanded, giving Hughes a hard look. Annie started fishing around in a tiny purse while Hughes pulled out his Massachusetts private investigator ID card. He handed it to the officer and said, "Look, I'm a PI from Boston working on a missing person case. While standing at the bar, I was attacked by a couple of baboons."

The officer stared at Hughes, then studied the ID. Annie handed over her driver's license.

"Who attacked you?" he asked. Hughes shrugged and looked over at Annie.

She said, "I think a couple of locals. They looked like

shore rats. For some reason, they didn't like Danny asking questions. All he did was show a picture to the bartender."

"A picture? Let me see it."

Hughes handed over the picture he had of Arnold. The police officer, young and probably a summer hire, blankly stared at it. "Never saw him," he said, handing it back. "Anyone pressing charges?"

Hughes looked at Annie. "No idea who the guys were or why they attacked us. I think we just want to leave." A deep ache was starting to run through his right arm from the sap hit. Blood from his cheek had dripped onto his white tee.

The cop shrugged. "Get the hell out of here. And probably get off the Jersey Shore."

Hughes took Annie's hand. "We're gone. Thanks, officer."

As they walked back to their cars, Annie took out a tissue from her purse and handed it to Hughes. He pressed it to his cheek. "How about a cup of coffee?" he asked.

"There's a diner just over the bridge. Might be good to sit for a while."

Hughes nodded.

The diner was all chrome and Formica, too brightly lit. Hughes was grateful for it, though. They settled into a booth. After a minute, the waitress, a blonde with dark roots who acted like her feet hurt, ambled over and stood holding a pad. They ordered coffee and waited for it to arrive. Hughes told the waitress that they would order food later; she spun around, heading to another booth. Annie took a sip of her coffee and looked directly at Hughes. "So, you want to tell me what that was all about?"

Hughes thought for a moment, then said, "I am supposed to be on a case to find a simple runaway.

Obviously, there is more to this story than I thought. Showing the photo pissed off those morons; no idea why."

"I've seen the big one before. I think he's a local wannabe."

"Wannabe, like in mob guys?"

"I don't know. He came into Anthony's a while back with a blonde who looked like a hooker. He had a wad of money and tipped me heavily. I didn't like his vibes."

Hughes was rubbing his arm, which was still numb. He took in Annie with a hint of sadness. "A. Treat, as much as I hate to say this, I've got to get back to Boston and my clients. I need to figure out what is going on. Sorry about this first date."

Annie shrugged and shifted in the booth. Hughes could see the small bumps from her nipples in her tee shirt. She then smiled. "Dan, you are a pretty exciting guy. I hope you come back soon."

The waitress returned and again stood with her pad. Hughes gave her a grin and ordered two omelets.

"So, tell me about yourself," Hughes asked while they waited.

"Not so different," she said. "Jersey girl. Married once to a Jersey boy. Typical guy who could not keep it in his pants. It lasted a little over a year, then he left me with a whole lot of bills. Been playing catch-up ever since. Been quite a while."

"No one in your life now?"

"Sure, a bunch of them. All pretty much the same. One FWB that I like and can talk to; otherwise just guys sitting at the bar. How about you?"

Hughes thought for a while, tempted to play the game, then decided she was too nice to BS. "Grew up in upstate New York and moved to the city when I was eighteen.

Went to NYU. Great times. Had no idea what I wanted to do, so I enlisted, got commissioned, and went into military intelligence. Spent almost four years as a counterintelligence officer. Finally moved to Boston. Decided being a PI was great fun and stayed with it. Most of the time, it is great fun."

"Even nights like tonight?"

The omelets arrived, and they grew quiet as they started into them.

After a minute, Hughes continued, "This is certainly out of the ordinary but, frankly, a lot of the stuff I do can result in some people getting pretty teed off. But so far, I've managed to stay out of harm's way. But not tonight." He rubbed his arm. "I thought this would be mostly a little vacation. Come to the Jersey Shore, find the kid, and bring him home. Maybe a couple of weeks, including some beach time. Now I don't know. I have to have a little chat with my clients."

"So, are you heading back to Boston?"

They ate slowly as they talked. The omelet was better than Hughes expected and Annie's conversation was smart and engaging. He liked her.

The diner filled up with clubbers dragging themselves in for something to line their stomachs with. A couple of the men yelled and shouted with raging testosterone. The waitress regarded them with undisguised scorn. The small hint of intimacy Hughes and Annie had swirled away in the tide of revelry.

Annie stared down at the remains of her meal. She was quiet, then looked up at Hughes and said in a little voice, "Want to come home with me?"

Hughes felt the surge of desire flow through him like a faucet was turned on. The coffee cup he was lifting stopped halfway, and he smiled as a way to find time. He looked into her large brown eyes and considered. Annie flushed and took a sip of her coffee. Hughes thought she was as delicious as fresh strawberry shortcake. He thought also of Angie.

After an awkward minute, he said, "Annie, my arm is still dead. If it's not better by morning, I'll have to find an ER. Might be better tonight to take it easy."

Annie straightened. "Sure, I don't blame you. Are you staying here much longer?"

"I think I better get back to my clients and figure out what is going on. Tonight is a shock. Depending on what I find out, I'll probably be back in a couple of days."

Annie looked somehow relieved. She recovered. "Hope you still will like Italian food. I'll be at the bar." She pushed her plate a couple of inches to the center of the table, a clear signal. Hughes got it and said, "Well, maybe we should get going. Late."

He signaled to the waitress, who was sitting at the counter, leaning on her elbow. She shuffled over to the booth and waited.

"Check," Hughes said. Then he said to Annie, "If you're not going back toward the Molly Pitcher, I think I can find my way."

The moment gone, she replied, "I'm going the other way. You sure you know where you are?"

"No problem."

The check arrived, and Hughes left money with a generous tip, rewarding the mediocre service. They made their way outside, past sagging, tired clubbers and into the humid summer night. The briny smell of the sea was strong. Hughes walked Annie to her car, and she paused while hitting the "unlock" button. Both could still feel the warm flow of desire. Hughes looked again into those eyes and said in a hoarse whisper, "Thanks for everything. You are really special."

She paused, then said, "Sure. Night. See you." A dismissal.

He stood next to the car as she started it and drove away across the parking lot. He turned and went to the Mustang parked ten feet away, physically rubbing his sore arm and mentally rubbing his libido.

There was no one at the desk when he returned to the inn. He let himself into the room and found a professional turndown with a small, round chocolate on the pillow.

Pulling off his tee, Hughes went into the bathroom and examined his arm in the mirror over the sink. An ugly bump was growing purple. He checked out his cheek and decided it was a minor scratch. He washed his face and caught the time on the bedside radio. Almost 3 a.m. Interesting night. Exhaustion poured over him like warm syrup. Standing at the window, staring at the black river, he thought about Annie Treat and what he could be doing instead.

What the fuck is the matter with me? he wondered, a combination of the case and Annie. Pulling off the rest of his clothes, he got into bed and was asleep in seconds.

By 7 a.m., he was up and staring at the slack-eyed face in the bathroom mirror. He threw cold water on his face and called Angie.

She answered after four rings, her voice breathy and heavy with sleep. "Danny?"

"Hi, babe," he said, not succeeding in an attempt to sound "up."

Quickly awake, she said, "Everything OK?"

"Well, a surprise last night. I started asking around,

looking for my subject, and two goons jumped me. No idea why. Either they didn't like my looks—something impossible to believe—or something about me asking about the guy I'm looking for."

"You OK?" Angie's voice was shrill and anxious.

"Yeah, I'm fine. I got nailed with a sap, but I was able to get my arm up. It took the hit. Sore but OK."

Angie was silent on the other end. Finally, "What are you going to do? How about bagging the case?"

"Not yet. I'm coming home to talk to my clients. Try to find out what's going on. How about dinner tonight at Atlantic Fish? I should be home by around three or four."

"How about me cooking Italian? The bar has a new Chianti. Sounds like you can use some comfort food."

"I'm on my way. Love ya," he said hanging up, feeling better about himself.

Hughes threw his bag together and headed out. Ginger Christmas was at the lobby desk and looked surprised to see him. "Leaving us so soon?" she asked, pouting.

"Yeah, I have to head home, at least for a while. Hope I will be back."

"Hope so. I'll run your bill right away."

While she was doing that, Hughes scanned the lobby, paranoid. In all of his cases, he's never been attacked like that. Never so blatant. Got to be a lot more that he didn't know.

Ginger smiled weakly and pushed the room receipt to him. "Be careful," she said, and Hughes wondered.

The Mustang was unperturbed and the satisfying growl as the engine caught gave him some confidence. He pulled out and headed north. Across the George Washington Bridge, New York City on his right, huge and shimmering like a mythical Oz, he picked up the Saw Mill River Parkway, then left on the Merritt.

In a comfortable cruise, Hughes thought about things. A simple runaway. Why? No idea. The lure of the Jersey Shore, the nude beach, the young women. Any number of reasons for a nineteen-year-old to bolt. A simple job. Find the moron; bring him home. So why would two goons get upset with me looking? Got to be more to the story.

With soft jazz on the radio, he let his mind drift.

Arnold had access to money. And it didn't sound like he was the most sophisticated kid in the world. So if some wise guys got their hooks into him, they may not like anyone snooping around to see what was going on.

Hughes made good time and parked the Mustang on Beacon Street. Boston seemed staid compared to where he was. The Jersey Shore wore its action like a fast sports car, Boston more like an elegant Bentley.

He made his way up the stairs to his second-floor apartment and let himself into a musty, airless space.

Should have left some windows open, he thought to himself.

He tossed down his bag, taking the .38 out, and placed it inside the nightstand. He felt clammy after the trip and pulled off his tee and jeans and headed into the shower. He let the cool water run over his head, enjoying the feeling, and never heard the key in the front door. His eyes were closed when the shower curtain was pulled open, startling him. Angie stepped in and was glistening in an instant. She looked at the purple lump on his arm, brought her lips to it, smiled up, and pulled close to him to get the full spray. He put his arms around her and together they let the water run.

Once out of the shower and calming down, Angie threw on a long tee shirt and headed for the kitchen. True to her word, she brought everything she needed for dinner, including two bottles of excellent Chianti.

Hughes lay down on the bed and let himself drift. The Jersey Shore case was perplexing.

The sweet smell of simmering tomato sauce wafted into the bedroom and pulled him out of his doze. He got up and looked at himself in the freestanding mirror in the corner. His shoulders were solid, and arms thick with muscle. Stomach flat with just a hint of love handles.

The scratch on his cheek was almost invisible, but his arm was still aching and the plum-colored bruise still angry. If he hadn't been fast enough to catch the sap on the arm, it may have done some serious damage.

Hughes pulled on a pair of blue running shorts and padded out into the kitchen. Angie was at the stove, stirring the sauce in a huge pot. The tee shirt came down to only halfway across her bottom. Hughes paused to admire the scene and thought how lucky he was. Less regret about Ms. Treat. There could not be a better ass than Angie's in the world.

Chapter 11

The next morning, they woke up to another scorcher. Angie discarded the tee shirt for a short silk robe with vague Japanese designs, which she wore open. She went to prepare coffee while Hughes went to his desk to list the questions he had for the client.

- How much money did the kid have access to?
- Did he have a pattern of running away?
- What is personality like?

Other questions came to him, helping to figure out exactly what he had gotten himself into.

His head was clearer, and he was anxious to get some answers.

"Coffee's ready," Angie called. "Want some breakfast?"

"Nah, I'm going to walk over to Marlboro Street and I'll get something at the Parish Café. Seems like a good day to sit on the outside deck and read the paper. I need to keep my mind clear and you are the worst one for me to do that," he said, getting up and heading for the kitchen.

She handed him a cup as he approached and he gave her a kiss on the cheek. "I love your outfit," he said.

"Hot today. Too bad I can't stay this way all day."

"You do and I'll never get anything done."

"But not that bad of a way to start the day." She warmly chuckled.

"Got that right." He gave her a soft pat on her behind and grinned stupidly at her. She stepped away, saying work was calling.

Hughes nodded and came back to his previous thought process.

"This case has got me perplexed. Why should a couple of goons attack someone looking for a runaway? Got to be more to this. I need to get the clients to clue me in."

Angie, letting the call go to her voicemail, shrugged. "I don't like you getting beat up. Maybe just drop the whole thing."

"Not in my character to cut and run. Besides, I owe payback to those assholes."

"Payback could be very bad. Don't forget you're dealing with New Jersey."

Hughes put his cup down and put his arms around her. "Nothing like a good woman worrying about you," he said.

"OK, tough guy, just be careful."

"I'll watch my back. I'll know better if I can get the Levines to spill what is going on."

Angie looked up at him and smiled. She squeezed his hands and snuggled in closer. Hughes felt good. He reluctantly pulled away and headed into the bedroom. He pulled on fresh jeans, a black short-sleeved shirt, and New Balance running shoes. He looked in the mirror and decided, despite the heat, to throw on a khaki summer sports jacket to look more professional for the Levines. Then he combed his thick, dark hair. Satisfied, he headed out, giving Angie a peck on the top of her head as she sat at the table checking her emails.

When he pushed open the lobby door onto Joy Street, early morning humidity hit him like a wet dishcloth. He headed down Beacon Street, dodging state office workers hurrying up the hill. As he crossed Charles Street and cut into the Public Garden, he fondly remembered a former fling who once brought champagne and strawberries to the Garden for him. It made for a charming and romantic picnic before she led him back to her Back Bay apartment.

The Garden was in full summer bloom. The tulips had passed, but myriad other varieties were making a Monet backdrop.

Hughes headed out on Boylston Street and was happy to find the outside deck of the Parish Café only half-full. With a Boston Globe from the newspaper vending machine, he found a small table in the corner. He could dawdle over coffee, read the paper, and covertly watch the young women in summer dresses.

Two cups of coffee and a fresh bagel with chive cream cheese later, Hughes tossed his paper into the trash and strode down Boylston Street. On the corner of Berkeley Street, two young blonde women were staring at a map of the city streets festooned with cartoon pictures. Both were wearing very short skirts and tube tops. Obviously not Bostonians and obviously lost. Hughes stopped and smiled.

"Hi, I'm Dan. Can I help?" he said. They looked startled, then smiled back.

In a heavy French accent, the taller of the two said, "Fanny Hall?"

Hughes thought for a moment, then realized, "Oh, you must mean Faneuil Hall. It's a little walk from here."

"Show us?" said the other girl, smiling, dimples appearing in her peach cheeks. She looked into Hughes's eyes.

"OK, head down the street," he said, pointing, "and cut across the Common. Up and over the hill and turn left and you're there."

Both girls were in deep concentration as he spoke. The taller girl, getting it, repeated the directions. They grinned at Hughes. "Merci, merci." Then they were off.

Hughes watched them go, skirts swishing in the light breeze and felt a familiar rush. Perfect.

He turned down Berkeley to Marlboro, another world just three blocks away. The din of traffic noise somehow faded away and leafy trees shaded the sidewalk. Already sweating, he made his way to the Levines' townhouse and banged the heavy door knocker. After a couple of minutes, the door opened and Ira Levine stared at him through thick glasses. He looked confused, then said, "Oh, Mr. Hughes. Did you find Arnold?"

"No, I have to talk to you about that. May I come in?"

"Oh, yes, of course." Then calling over his shoulder, "Sara, that detective is here."

Hughes stepped into the foyer, which smelled of wet leaves, and waited. After a minute, Sara Levine yelled down to come up. Ira smiled at him and led the way upstairs to the parlor. Sara was standing there in what seemed like the same billowing dress she had worn the first time they had met. She grimaced. "Did you find Arnold?"

"No, Mrs. Levine. I started looking on the Jersey Shore and, without warning, I was attacked by two guys who apparently didn't like me asking about him. Not the kind of thing I would expect for a runaway case. Is there something I don't know?"

Sara looked at Ira, who gave a small shrug, then let out a quiet sigh and said, "Well, our attorney called. Arnold has been tapping into his trust fund quite a bit. We can't imagine where that money is going. That's why we wanted you to find him."

"When you say tapping it quite a bit, how much is 'quite a bit'?"

Sara looked at her husband. "How much do we think, Ira?"

Ira mumbled something, then went to a rolltop desk in the corner, opened it, and pulled out what appeared to be a ledger book. He thumbed through it and finally said, "Looks like he took out about twenty-nine thousand dollars last month, a little less the month before."

Hughes looked at Sara, who was impassive. "About how much in total since he's been gone?"

Ira checked his book again. "Well, at first there was not much at all. The first couple of weeks he was gone, he took out about twelve hundred dollars. Then the withdrawals got much larger. About sixty-five thousand has been taken out so far."

"In a little more than three months? Those are a lot of cheeseburgers. Any idea where the money is going? Was any sent to a specific place or person?"

Ira looked embarrassed. "No, it is always for cash and seems like a lot is going into an account we haven't been able to identify."

Hughes looked at Ira, then Sara. Both were silent. "No idea where the money is going?" he asked.

They both shook their heads slightly.

"Why didn't you tell me this before?" Hughes asked.

Sara said, "We didn't want you to think Arnold was bad

or doing something he shouldn't be doing. We just wanted him home so we could ask him ourselves."

"Not to overdramatize this, but I think Arnold's into something a lot more than running away to go to the beach. The two guys who attacked me did so for a reason. Sixty-five thousand dollars—that's a pretty good reason. Do you think he would give the money to someone voluntarily?"

Faces blank, the Levines didn't answer.

"I take that as a no."

Ira took Sara's hand, which she wrenched away. She glared at Hughes. "Are you quitting on us? Don't think we will pay for nothing."

She made the air inside the room thick.

"I'm not thinking about quitting. I've got a lot of money invested, not to mention some serious bruises. I'll find your Arnold and bring him back if possible, but I've got to know what I'm walking into. Now let's sit down and get honest with each other."

Ira said, "I'll make some tea."

Sara stood motionless like a piece of furniture covered for storage. It was hard to read her expression, anger tinged with deep indifference. Hughes studied her for another minute, then said, "I think I'll sit down. I have a feeling there is much to learn."

She said nothing as she sat in a frayed wingback chair across the room, continuing to glare at Hughes.

Minutes later, Ira shuffled into the room carrying a tray containing a white-and-blue porcelain teapot with three tiny cups on saucers. He put the tray down on the coffee table and poured the tea into the cups. He offered one to Hughes, who accepted it with a quiet thank you, but Sara ignored the service.

"OK," Hughes said, "let's start at the beginning. How does Arnold have access to that money?"

Ira looked at Sara, who remained inert like a sphinx, then said quietly, "Well, Sara's father, Ivan, created this trust fund after we adopted Arnold and set it up so that we had no access to it. Arnold was eligible to withdraw funds from it at age eighteen."

"How much money is in the trust fund?"

Ira looked at Sara, who gave a slight nod. "We understand there is just under two million dollars."

The silence was palatable. Then Hughes said, "And he has complete access to it?"

"Well, it is his money," Ira replied.

Sara cut in. "It's his money, but we are entitled to it as well. We raised him. Put him through schools, fed him, and paid the lawyers when he got into trouble. Arnold was always a bit of trouble. He ran away from two schools and was expelled from two. He came down with a bad case of gonorrhea and was accused several times of doing drugs. It's as much ours as his."

"Your father, Ivan, what does he think?" Hughes asked.

Ira responded for his wife. "He's very ill. Sometimes doesn't know where he is. We're worried about him."

Hughes said, "And worried he will make sure you get none of that money." He looked back and forth between the two of them. "So Arnold turns eighteen and gets access to enough money to get him into trouble. Is that when he took off?"

"We tried to reason with him. Asked him for a power of attorney so we could make sure the money was used for good. He got kind of crazy and yelled at us. Said horrible things," Ira mumbled.

"So he took off after that?"

Sara jumped in. "He calmed down, and we were hoping he would be reasonable. But a week after that, he was gone. Hardly anything of his was taken. He just seemed to disappear. We were hoping he would just come back. He didn't have any friends that we knew about. Never had a girlfriend. He had nowhere to go."

Ira said, "After he was gone about three or four weeks, our attorney called and said Arnold was taking large sums of money out of his trust and asked if we knew about it. We had no idea."

Hughes wondered out loud, "What would Arnold be doing with the money?"

"We can't figure that out," Ira said. "He never collected much. He just read a lot and was alone a lot. He never asked for much. So we can't understand why the money is being taken out."

"I think it's pretty obvious there are other people involved," Hughes said. "Especially after my welcoming committee. Not to alarm you, but I think it's critical you get him back as soon as possible and away from whoever he's involved with."

Both Ira and Sara sat quietly. Ira looked like he had just eaten some bad fish—Sara like she wanted to strangle someone. The dim street noise was the only audible sound in the aging townhouse. After a minute, Hughes broke the silence. "Give me a thousand-dollar advance, and I'll go back. If I can't find him in a week, I'll return to Boston, and you can find someone else to search." He stood and waited. Sara nodded and turned to Ira. "Make the check out," she said curtly.

As Ira went to an antique secretary in the corner and pulled out a checkbook, Hughes stood and waited. Sara eyed him with contempt. Ira wrote out the check and handed it to Hughes, who placed it into his breast pocket without looking.

Hughes then said, "OK, I'll go back. The fact that I was attacked in the first place I looked is a good lead. There are more clubs to search, but I think that's how I can find him. Bringing him back may be another matter, but we can cross that bridge when we come to it."

Both Ira and Sara stared at him, not saying a word. The old house creaked as a heavy vehicle could be heard passing by outside. The air inside was still and musty.

Hughes headed to the stairs and out the front door into a humid and hot Boston that smelled like cut grass. He walked up Marlboro Street and turned onto Dartmouth, lost in thought. It looked like some bad guys were taking Arnold's trust fund money, either with or without his permission. In either case, it stunk with at least manipulation, if not extortion. This time, he would approach the case differently.

Hughes turned left on Boylston, this time paying no attention to the young women in their summer dresses on the street. He decided to stop back at the Parish Café to sit and think. He found a corner table on the outside deck. Thin waves of heat rose from the blacktop of the street. After a minute, a young woman in a short, black skirt and white tee approached and smiled by way of greeting.

Hughes, distracted, looked up indifferently and said, "How about a muffin and coffee?"

"Sure, be back in a minute."

As she moved away, he stared out to the street and thought about the case. At an angle, he could see a boutique displaying twelve-hundred-dollar Hermes scarves and, a little further down, slick, expensive cars driving into the Four Seasons hotel entrance. It was now obvious the Levines had little understanding of their ward.

Arnold's origin was indeed mysterious. From their description of their adopted son, he was quiet and introverted with little street smarts. Someone in New Jersey was getting hold of his money, most likely involuntarily if the attack in the beach bar was any indication. How to find Arnold was one thing. How to bring him back was another. Hughes figured he would need help.

After one bite, he left the muffin on the table, along with the coffee and a five-dollar bill, and headed out. The waitress watched him from across the deck.

He cut across the Public Garden and onto Joy Street. As he headed up the stairs to his apartment, he had a lot of it sorted out. Angie would help immensely.

The apartment was surprisingly cool, and he tossed his jacket over the back of a chair and pulled off his tee, which was damp from the walk. He headed in for a cool shower, which cleared his head. He came out with a towel wrapped around his waist, then went to lie down on the couch.

As part of a personal meditation, he started relaxing his body, starting from his toes and working up. By the time he got to his face, he started drifting off to sleep. With a start, he felt his towel being pulled off. Tensing, he woke to see Angie standing over him, grinning.

"A girl will never know what she might find after shopping. I was out looking for new shorts and found a naked Adonis instead."

Hughes felt an involuntary excitement starting. "Oops, I better find those shorts," he said.

"Good idea."

He grabbed the towel and headed into the bedroom.

After pulling on white summer pants, he returned. "I've been thinking. Can you get away to New Jersey with me?"

Angie headed to the refrigerator and pulled out a bottle of Snapple ice tea. "What's the matter? No talent on the Shore for you?" she said without turning around.

"Angie, this case I took on is a lot more complicated than I thought and I need some help. How about we head out for an early dinner so we can talk over a glass of wine?"

"Sounds good to me, sugar. Let me shower up and change. Give me an hour and we can get that wine."

Hughes pulled on a black, lightweight shirt and a pair of tan loafers with no socks. The khaki sports jacket was still on the chair where he had tossed it and was in decent shape. He went to his desk and started making notes about the case, trying to get as much detail from memory about the incident on the Shore. Angie emerged from the bedroom a little later wearing a short, floral summer dress and lace-up sandals. Her legs were nice and tan.

"Ready," she said.

They walked back across the Common and Public Garden; the sun was an oversized pumpkin, making the tops of the buildings golden. They turned onto Newbury Street and found an outside table at 29 Newbury. Angie ordered a chardonnay, Hughes a Sam Adams beer. The thin, handsome waiter practically pranced away when they said they needed some time before ordering dinner.

"So," Angie started, taking a sip of her chilled wine, "what's going on with this mess you've gotten yourself into again?"

"Turns out, little Arnold is not just some spoiled runaway; he's got access to a seven-figure trust fund. And somehow the fund is being emptied at an alarming rate. He's been reclusive and withdrawn, so probably vulnerable to predators. And, believe me, I've seen some vicious-looking predators on the Jersey Shore."

"Predators on the Jersey Shore? Why am I not surprised?" Angie glanced up at an attractive couple walking by, both in summer linens.

"So," Hughes continued, also watching the couple as they passed, "someone has gotten their clutches into Arnold and his bucks. It may be a woman, but I doubt it. The gorillas who attacked me didn't look anything like jealous boyfriends. Most likely, some heavies have gotten their claws into him, either through intimidation, fear, or fake friendship. I'm guessing the former."

Angie thought for a minute. "How am I supposed to help?"

"I need a diversion. Someone they look at while I make some maneuvers behind them."

She took a larger sip and stared into the glass. "So, I'm sort of bait?"

Hughes looked at her with concern. "Yeah, I guess so," he said.

Angie shrugged. "OK, let's do it. Sunshine, sea, and beach mixed in with stupid danger. What else could a girl ask for?"

The waiter was eyeing them from the corner. Hughes grinned at Angie, then signaled him over. They ordered a Caesar salad and burger to be split between them and another round of drinks. While they waited for the food, Hughes went into detail about his trip, the Molly Pitcher Inn, the Shore, and beach bar, skimming over details about Annie Treat.

Angie ate silently, nodding from time to time as she pictured what had transpired so far. When the meal was finished, they sat quietly and watched the street traffic for a moment.

Angie said, "OK, this is complicated. I still don't know what you have in mind to succeed."

"I don't either. I will play it as it goes along."

"As you usually do. Will that be good enough in this case?"

"Has to be. No Plan A or B yet. Come on, I'll walk us home. Too nice an evening to worry."

The sky grew heavy with the threat of rain. The humidity rose. They walked slowly into the Public Garden, feeling the change in the air. They were quiet for several minutes, then Angie asked, "Dan, do you ever think about getting out of your business? I mean, it can be dangerous, and what are you going to do when you get older?"

"Sometimes," he said. "But there is so much fun from day to day, I never really think about it. I never ceased to be amazed by human nature. Seems like every day is a surprise. Think about what we are getting into. The runaway, Arnold, is the result of god knows what kind of relationship. Is he screwed up or are his adopted parents?"

"But there's no continuity. You are always looking for the next job. Maybe it comes, maybe not."

"I know. Maybe I'll finish in a while and write my memoirs. But it seems more like it chose me rather than me choosing what I'm doing."

Angie smiled at him, then shook her head in mild amusement.

Raindrops, like small pieces of crystal from a chandelier, started to fall. They quickened their pace, heading up the Boston Common steps to Beacon Street. It started to pour just as they dashed into the front foyer of his apartment building on Joy Street, both laughing. Upstairs, they dried off. Hughes sat at his small desk to make out a plan while Angie put on coffee.

When it was ready, she brought two heavy mugs over, and they sat at the window, watching and listening to the rain, sipping coffee. Outside, some caught in the downpour seemed to relish it, letting themselves get soaked as they splashed in the puddles along the sidewalk. Despite the anxiety about the upcoming trip, Hughes felt close to Angie.

After a while, Hughes decided to pack, and Angie did the same. Just shorts, sandals, and tees, perfect for the trip to the Jersey Shore. Hughes slid his Airweight .38 back into his bag with a belt holster. After some thought, he also threw in an extra box of ammunition. Then a couple of long summer shirts to be worn outside to cover the piece on a belt.

They went to bed early, watching the Discovery Channel on the bedroom TV until both fell asleep.

Chapter 12

Early the next morning, sharp sunlight streamed through the grime on the window. The sound of going-to-work traffic seeped into the quiet room like the breathing of a distant machine. Angie got up first, heading to the kitchen for coffee, the tee shirt she was wearing not quite covering her bottom.

Hughes stretched and went to the window. The sun was slanting through the trees in the Boston Common. The smell of brewing coffee got him moving, and he headed into the bathroom for a shower. Letting the cool water pour over his head, he heard Angie pad into the bathroom.

"Morning, sunshine," she said. "Coffee is on the sink. Leave the water running and I'll jump in when you're finished."

"You can jump in right now if you want."

"I thought you wanted to get on the road for our big adventure. No time for frolics."

"Killjoy," he replied. "I'm finishing up. It's all yours."

As he stepped out of the shower, Angie jumped in, generating a pleasant rush in him as she pushed by him.

He toweled off and pulled on lightweight cotton slacks and a black tee shirt. Hair still wet, he headed out and down Beacon Street to the deli. When he got back with a bottle of fresh orange juice and two raspberry Danish pastries, Angie was already dressed and putting on light makeup in front of the bathroom mirror. She was wearing khaki shorts, a sports bra, a white tee shirt, and high-top canvas shoes. Hughes thought she looked like she was going on a safari.

"With you, every day is a safari, buster," she mocked.

"OK, let's get on the road," he said. She put on a Red Sox ball cap and took a cup of coffee to go.

Hughes eyed the cap. "I see you are in disguise."

"Are you kidding?" she said. "All the world's a Sox fan. I'll fit right in."

Hughes grinned.

They headed out and turned up to Mount Vernon Street, where the Mustang sat under ancient trees in front of a way-too-charming townhouse. He tossed the luggage into the trunk, and they settled into the leather. The car responded immediately.

"Danny, the car sounds like it wants to go."

"OK. Off we go to thwart the forces of evil."

"Thwart?"

"Yep, that's us. Thwarters."

He shifted into first and headed down the leafy and picturesque street. They picked up the Mass Turnpike West and exited onto Route 85 south past Hartford, picking up the Merritt Parkway fifteen minutes later.

Angie settled back in her seat. There was soft jazz on the radio. Traffic was thick with vans and SUVs full of families and summer vacation gear. Hughes noticed that several of the male drivers looked twice at Angie when they passed them.

Angie watched the Connecticut countryside slide by.

"You know," she said, "the woods in this state are really beautiful. Clean and fresh. And I love the overpasses. Many have these elegant carvings on them."

"Wait until you see the Jersey Shore again," he said.

Two hours into the trip, Angie said, "Dan, is there anything you're not telling me about this assignment. You still have a bruise on your arm. You normally don't get attacked when doing a locate."

He thought for a minute. "Don't know. It's not a simple runaway. The family is as dysfunctional as a eunuch in a brothel. We have to find our guy and get him back to Boston. I figure we'll work on the second part when we find out what his problem is and who is so sensitive about someone looking for him. Initially, I think you can just watch my back. If you can help more, we'll know later on."

"Don't like the feel of this. It's not like the bar spottings we do so often. And New Jersey has a reputation."

Hughes rolled on some power and swung the car around a van ambling along with a canoe on top. The driver had a ball cap on backward, and the woman in the passenger seat had her hair piled high on top. He stared at Angie as the Mustang went by.

"I know," Hughes said. "Guess I need you mostly for moral support."

"That's not me," she said. "Supporting morals."

There was a tie-up halfway down the Merritt. While they sat in traffic, Hughes opened the top. Angie pulled on her Red Sox cap and stretched, smiling at him.

Chapter 13

The smell of seaweed baking in the sun mixed in with the salt air. Although it was early, the beach was starting to fill up.

Arnold Levine slowly drifted back to consciousness after a night of sleeping on a ratty and torn couch. His mouth was dry, and he licked his cracked lips as he sat up. His stained tee shirt and shorts hung on him like wet laundry.

As he started to focus, the screen door banged open. A young woman, blonde with dark roots and soft around her middle, stared at him.

"God, you look like shit," she said as Bobby Musa came in from the kitchen.

"Hi, babes," he said. "Arnie, say hello to Tiffany. Doesn't she look good in that tank top and shorts?"

"Hi, Tiffany" was all he was able to say. Then, "Hungry."

"Not to worry. Papa Bobby has some burgers and hot dogs on the grill out back."

Tiffany continued to stare at Arnold. "Jesus, Bobby. Shouldn't we toss him into the ocean? He smells."

"He'll clean up pretty soon. Won't you, Arnie?" Then to Tiffany, "Come into the kitchen. I want to talk to you."

"The kitchen? Usually, it's the bedroom."

"Later, babes. Right now I want to talk. Arnie, hang out here; we'll be right back. Maybe change your tee shirt."

A loud female yelp followed by a male laughing came from the beach, signaling a growing crowd. The air in the house remained cool and musty.

Inside the kitchen, Tiffany wrinkled up her nose at the stack of filthy dishes in and around the sink. "What is it, Bobby? You gonna show me how well you clean up?"

He grinned at her. "Check this out."

He went to the dented refrigerator and opened the top freezer. From there, he pulled out a frozen pizza box and placed it on the table. Opening one side, he pulled out several small styrene bags.

"Holy fuck. Is that what I think it is?" She glanced back at the living room, where she could hear Arnold shuffling around.

"High-grade H," he said. "Not for you, babes. I need you lucid when we get started. It's for your little friend in the living room."

"Jesus," she whispered. "Where did you get it?"

Putting it back in the box and the box back into the freezer, he said, "I got contacts. It's what keeps the piggy bank open." He put one thick arm around Tiffany, bringing her in to him. He pulled down her tube top, her breasts standing out, nipples already hard. He gave each one a quick kiss.

"Really?" she said.

"Nope, not now. Let's go chat with my boy, Arnie. Pull up your top. We don't want to get him too excited."

Arnold was standing at the front window watching beachgoers in blazing colors pass. Musa smiled at him as he turned. Tiffany also gave a weak smile. She looked around the room for a place to sit, recoiling from the couch, and finally settling into an overstuffed chair by the front window.

"So, Arnold, how's it going?" she asked.

He turned to her. He looked somehow hollow. "OK, but I'm hungry," he mumbled. She noted his skinny arms were pockmarked.

"Bobby, you going to the Pony tonight?" Tiffany scratched at her side and arms.

"Yeah. Probably. Some of the guys should be there."

The heat inside the house rose noticeably.

"Arnie, let's clean up a little and eat some lunch. Then I need you to log into your computer again," Musa said.

Arnold looked startled. "Bobby, again? You got some money just yesterday, I think." His voice was faint.

"You know I need to buy some of your supplies," Musa chuckled. "I know you're going to ask me for some later on."

Arnold shrugged.

"Now I need you to go into the bedroom and wash up a little and change your clothes. Tiffany, go with him."

She made a face and shivered but followed Arnold.

Outside, the day warmed with only a mild breeze that did nothing to temper the heat. A powerful Ferrari rumbled passed, turning away at the corner. A couple walked by. He was pulling a cart with huge rubber wheels that was packed with beach gear. She was wearing a white straw hat and an oversized blue shirt that said "NY Giants." But, inside, the house reeked of mold and human stink.

Chapter 14

Traffic on the Garden State was awful, so they were not able to pull into the Molly Pitcher Inn until the middle of the afternoon. The circular driveway had a couple of sedans and vans parked in a row.

Hughes, able to pull in directly at the front entrance, popped open the trunk and escorted Angie into the cool of the lobby. The white marble floor, set off by the large ferns in the corners, gave a sophisticated elegance. A touch of Bogey and Bacall.

At the front desk, Ginger Christmas was working. She eyed Hughes, then Angie, and sighed.

"Back so soon?" she asked as she pushed the sign-in register across the counter. Angie stood back a few paces and eyed the expansive lobby broken up by large leather chairs in sitting groups. She nodded in approval.

"Yep, not sure how long we'll be here. Hard to leave the Jersey Shore this time of the year."

"I love it," she replied. I've got you into a nice king-size on the ground floor. It has a small balcony and overlooks the river. Very pretty."

Hughes gave her a small smile as he took the keys. "Thanks, Ginger," he said and glanced around and found their luggage sitting behind him. He forced a non-flirt glance back at her and headed toward the other side of the lobby.

The room was nicely appointed, and when Hughes pulled open the curtains, the view from the small balcony was stunning. A few people lounged in the pool below them with the marina beyond. Angie went to the large window, stared outside at the marina, and stretched. She turned and plopped onto the king-size bed.

"Oh, comfy," she murmured. "Are we in a rush?"

Hughes was unpacking his duffel and turned to see her grinning at him from the bed.

"We have lots of time. The plan is to head out and scour some of the clubs, and they won't wake up until after ten o'clock. All we have to do is have dinner before."

"Is that all we have to do?"

The afternoon light put the room in a soft focus. "I can think of something else," he said. Angie bounced up from the bed, pulling off her tee shirt, revealing her large sports bra. "I want to clean off the road dust. Going in to shower."

"OK," Hughes said. He stared out the window, thinking how different the scene at the marina below, with the white runabouts and nautical flags, was from the beach bars on the Shore.

A couple of minutes later, Angie came out from the bathroom wrapped in a thick, white towel. She pulled the covers down on the bed, letting the towel drop at the same time.

Hughes grinned, taken by the contrast of the tanned to the untanned portions of her body.

"I think you need to work on your tan lines, honey. Maybe we should make a trip to the Gunnison nude beach."

Rolling over, she said, "I don't know. I was there a couple of years ago and the place was filled with strange characters. You won't believe what can be pierced."

"Whatever. Plenty to do here," he said, pulling off his shirt.

The sun was a shimmering pumpkin as it dropped toward the horizon. Hughes and Angie were coming back from light naps.

She stretched, got up, and went to the window. "Wow," she said. "Beautiful. But I'm getting hungry. Is it getting time for dinner?"

"I'm famished, too. There's a pretty good Italian place right across the street. There's a great bartender there who helped me out the first time around. Let's go meet her and get dinner."

"I'll be the judge of the Italian food and the bartender, so be careful with your compliments, buster."

There was no perceptive drop in temperature as they made their way across the road to Anthony's. The summer air was mixed with the smell of soft blacktop.

Chapter 15

A s Hughes and Angie were relaxing away from the heat of midday, Musa was heating a spoon over the stove. Tiffany watched with mild curiosity, idling scratching her arm. He dropped a small amount of the cream-colored powder onto the spoon and watched it melt and start to bubble. He grinned at Tiffany.

"Go get the piggy bank," he said, motioning with a nod of his head. Tiffany headed out of the kitchen to where Arnold was seated, staring out the window. His arms stuck out like skinny sticks, pasty white. She stopped and studied him for a minute, almost starting to feel sorry for him.

"Hurry up," Musa yelled from the kitchen, breaking her thought.

"Come on, Arnie," she said, taking him by one of his weak arms. He looked up at her with vacant eyes and shakily stood up. She led him into the kitchen where Musa was concentrating on the boiling substance. Glancing over to Arnold, he took out a syringe and pulled the plunger up until the barrel was filled halfway with the heroin.

"Arnie, we're going out tonight and this will help you have a good time. But before we leave, I need you to transfer a little money for tonight's festivities. Maybe around two grand."

Arnold stared, fixated by the needle. "I don't know, Bobby. I'm tired and don't feel like going out."

"That's because you haven't eaten in a day or so. I'm grilling up some burgers. You'll feel a lot better when we're through. Just make sure you do the transfer correctly. If the bank calls like before, you know what to say."

Arnold nodded indifferently and stood inert.

Musa flicked at the needle, holding it vertical. He then pumped a drop out of it. "Come here, Arnie," he said, smiling.

Arnold stood solid, a wooden Indian. Finally, he took two steps forward. Musa gestured for him to sit down, and when he did, Musa picked up Arnold's left foot, holding it gingerly and with distaste. He then stuck the needle between Arnold's big and second toes. There was the slightest flinch.

Almost immediately, Arnold reacted, visibly relaxing with a sigh.

"Holy shit," Tiffany said, watching. "That's some powerful shit."

"Only the best for our guy here," Musa muttered. "How ya doin', buddy?" he asked.

Arnold gave a weak smile. "I'm OK. I want to go to the beach."

Musa turned to Tiffany. "Why don't you walk him to the beach and sit with him for a while? Do you both good."

She stared at him incredulously. "Are you fuckin' crazy? Sit on the beach with the zombie?"

Arnold took a step toward her. "I'm no zombie. And I like the beach."

Musa gave Tiffany a hard stare. "I said take him to the

beach. Stay away from the crowds. And wear a bathing suit that won't get you arrested. And buy him a hot dog and a Coke."

"OK, OK," she said. "We'll go for a little while. Come on, Arnie. You could use some sun." She pulled off her tube top, her breasts heavy and white. She searched in her bag for a bathing suit top and put on a yellow one she found, pushing and adjusting. Musa watched with mild lust. She lit a cigarette and winked at Musa. "You better hope no one better comes along. I may not come back."

"You'll be back, baby. If you know what's good for you. Just take care of our friend. Take a nap on the beach and be back here by four o'clock. We have to eat something and get ready for the Pony."

Before they left for the beach, Musa gave Arnold his cell phone and told him to dial. Within four minutes, two thousand dollars was transferred from Arnold's account into one Musa had set up under a bogus company name. The debit card he had under the company name would supply everything he would need during the night.

Outside, the soft summer day grew hot and sultry. The chatter and laughter from the beach sounded like a chorus of exotic birds.

Tiffany stared into her knockoff Gucci bag and pulled out a can of sunscreen. She shook it near her ear, then tossed it back into the bag. Her breasts almost spilled out her top as she bent over.

Arnold watched her with indifference. "I need something to drink," he said. A sour stink seeped off him.

She picked up her beach bag, slung it over her shoulder, and grinned at Arnold. "Come on, sugar, let's get some rays. And you can use a dip in the ocean. Closest thing you'll get to a bath today." She plopped a cap on his head, took his hand, and led him out the door.

Musa watched them shuffle down the street toward the beach entrance. He then went out back to the rubble-strewn yard, sat in the plastic chair there, and punched in a number on his cell phone.

"Yeah" was the answer after several rings.

"Bobby Musa, here. I want you to know that everything is working fine. The piggy bank is alive and well."

There was silence on the other end. So he continued, "I'll need another delivery by Tuesday. Same place, same price."

After a moment, "Price has gone up. Bring 10% more."

"Jesus. I'm already paying top dollar. Give me a break. We're all on the same side."

"Get another source, asshole."

"OK, I'm good for it," Musa replied. "I'll leave it in the same place."

The call disconnected. He got up and shook his head.

But he thought, *What the fuck. My profit is still good, and I'll just squeeze Arnie for more.*

He smiled to himself and lit a joint. *Life is good.*

Chapter 16

Hughes pulled on white cotton slacks with a black silk tee, then noticed Angie was wearing white pants and a dark-blue tee shirt. "We've got to stop looking like bookends," he said.

Angie smiled. "I thought of it first. You're the one who's imitating me."

Hughes gave her a pat on her bottom as she bent over to pull on high-heel sandals. "Thanks, I needed that," she said.

Hughes sat on the bed and put on a pair of New Balance running shoes. She watched him and said, "Planning on running away?"

"Nope, just need to be quick on my feet."

"OK, let's be quick and get to a restaurant. I'm starved."

The lobby was quiet with only a family of four checking in.

Ginger Christmas wished Hughes and Angie a pleasant evening with studied indifference. Hughes nodded back.

Across the street, the red "Anthony's" sign lit up the street like a setting sun.

The cool interior hit them like an open refrigerator door as they walked into the dark of the restaurant. Hughes spotted Annie Treat behind the bar and gave her a wave. She smiled at first, then put on a professional look as she saw Angie with him.

"Hi," Hughes said to her as he slid onto a barstool. "This is Angie. Angie, this is Annie Treat."

Annie gave a wide smile and stuck out her hand. "Welcome to the Shore," she said. "You have an exciting guy, there. I take him out on a tour and the next thing I know is he's being attacked by a couple of goons."

"Yep." Angie smiled. "He sure knows how to show a girl a good time."

There was a nice and instant rapport between the two women.

"What can I get you guys?" Annie asked, putting down two paper place mats on the bar.

Despite the high season, the restaurant was only slightly populated, including two couples who were not together.

Hughes said, "Bring me the best veal dish tonight with penne on the side."

"Sure," Annie said, turning to Angie. "What do you feel like? We have a nice striped bass tonight."

"If it's grilled, that would be terrific. Just that with a small veggie on the side."

"Perfect. How about some grilled asparagus with the bass? Maybe a glass of wine?"

Angie asked for a very chilled sauvignon blanc. Hughes asked for a Ketel One martini on the rocks.

When Annie disappeared into the kitchen, Hughes turned over one of the paper mats and started drawing a crude map. "We're here, and the road swings over toward the beach through the town of Rumson. You'll like Rumson."

Angie watched with mild amusement at his drawing.

"Then the road runs south along the ocean. All I can think to do is stop in as many bars and see if there is any sign of our long-lost runaway."

"Barhopping on the Jersey Shore. How do I get this kind of job?"

Annie came back with a basket of freshly baked rolls that smelled like a Saturday morning.

Turning to Angie, Annie said, "Did he tell you all the details about his welcoming party?"

"Are you kidding? He claimed he couldn't move his arm. Probably just an excuse not to cook or clean."

"Still no idea who those guys were?" Hughes asked.

"No, except they were not nice. In case you haven't heard, there are quite a few guys in Jersey who are not nice. Ever watch 'The Sopranos'?"

"That's why Angie's here. Someone's got to protect me."

Angie rolled her eyes. "Some big-time, big-deal private eye, eh?"

Annie grinned. Sisters in understanding.

The food arrived on time and was delicious. Annie chatted with them in between serving other customers. Both she and Hughes were silently grateful for their previous good judgment.

"I think we should start where I was before, at the Beachcomber," Hughes said. "Think so, Annie?"

She rolled her eyes. "Glutton for punishment. If you're still looking for that kid, I guess it's as good a place to start as any. There's also a new place, Jimmy's, across the street that's popular. Try there, too."

"We've got to be lucky as well as good," Hughes said, then asked for a coffee. Annie suggested another wine for

Angie, but she declined, still slowly sipping at her original glass.

As Hughes was paying the check, Annie looked at him, her face a mask of concern. "You guys are great. Be really careful out there. Anything I can do to help, let me know," she said.

"Thanks, Annie. Appreciate it. Let you know. I hope all the people on the Shore are as terrific as you."

"Hardly. Keep your head down. Watch over him, Angie."

"Good luck with that," Angie replied. "It's like trying to change the weather. I have a feeling we'll be back again soon."

When Hughes and Angie stepped back out onto Riverside Avenue, a glowing dusk was rapidly drawing into a full dark. The temperature had not dropped significantly, and the humid air smelled of dried flowers with a hint of the bay only a couple of blocks away.

They walked across the road to where the Mustang sat in the side parking lot. They smiled wanly at each other as they got into the car, each apprehensive as to what was coming up. Hughes started the car and placed the top down. Angie stared up at the front façade of the inn. "OK, onto our adventure," she said softly.

Hughes drove out of the lot and onto the avenue, turning left toward the center of Red Bank. Turning right onto Main Street, the village was quiet, despite the season. Most of the shops were already closed with only one sidewalk café open, half-populated with attractive young people. Remembering his trip with Annie Treat, Hughes found the way onto Rumson Road. As they exited Red Bank, the older but neat bungalows gradually morphed into larger homes. The front lawns got larger until some were fairway size.

As they cruised along, the mansions became more and more impressive, set back behind professionally tended flower beds. Angie mumbled to herself, "Old houses, old money."

Hughes glanced over at her and liked the Red Sox cap she was wearing with the wind ruffling her hair along the edges. Her olive skin looked flawless, and Hughes thought she was stunning with the dashboard lights reflecting on her face.

Entering Sea Bright, Hughes turned right and pulled into the front parking lot of the Beachcomber. Angie strained to see the main bar. "Is this where you had your encounter?"

"Yep. Gunfight at the Beachcomber corral."

"Looking forward to seeing the Earp brothers again?"

"Let's see. We'll take a look first at the beach bar, then peek into the main bar. We're early, so I don't expect a lot of people."

Hughes was right. As they took the stairs down to the beach bar, they could see only a couple of guys sitting around it, drinking beer from bottles. None Hughes recognized from before. They stood on the ocean side of the bar as they waited for a muscular bartender wearing a tee shirt that said "Rutgers" on it. He was deeply tanned and had long creases on the sides of his face testifying to his days in the sun. He didn't smile. "What'll you have?" he asked.

"Two Coronas and some information," Hughes said, placing two twenties on the bar. "What's your first name?"

The bartender grabbed two bottles from under the bar

and eyed them suspiciously. He aggressively stuck slices of lime in the tops of the bottles. "Mike," he said.

Angie smiled at the bartender as Hughes took out a photo of Arnold Levine. "Mike, I'm trying to help out a family. They haven't heard from their son in a while and are worried." He placed the photo on the bar between the two bottles of beer. "Any chance you've seen this kid around?"

Mike studied the photo for a minute. "Could have. Not sure. See a lot of stupid kids here. Don't think I can help you."

"OK, how about the main bar?" Hughes asked.

"You could try. Lot's more action up there. This kid a runaway or something?"

"Yeah, something," Hughes said.

The bartender shrugged and, taking the two twenties with him, moved away to two young women who came to the other side of the bar.

"Let's try at the main bar," Hughes said, looking around at the five people at the beach bar.

"OK, but I don't know if I can protect you," Angie said half-serious.

They came in from the back and saw a steady line of young people, all apparently in a party mood, streaming into the bar. Three bartenders were cutting fruit and serving the gathering crowd in rapid fashion. Hughes scanned the customers at the bar and did not see the heavies who had accosted him before. He led Angie to the near end of the bar and waited for a bartender, thick with a hanging gut, approach. "Yeah," he said by way of greeting.

"Couple of Coronas."

The ice-cold bottles were served immediately, and eight dollars was requested.

"Sure," said Hughes, putting a twenty on the bar. "By the way, ever see this guy?" he asked, putting the tattered photo on the bar. The bartender looked at Hughes like a mongoose eyeing a cobra, then looked down at the photo. He studied it for a minute, then said, "Never saw him," before walking away.

"Danny, are you thinking what I'm thinking?" Angie whispered.

"Yeah. He recognized the picture but won't say anything. I think, for some reason, this bar is a dead end for us. Let's get out of here."

Across the road was Jimmy's, a low, gray box structure with tables under umbrellas in front lending some color. The gravel parking lot on the left side was filling rapidly. Hughes felt taking the car out of the Beachcomber lot was a good idea, so they drove across the road and parked at the far end of the lot at Jimmy's.

They walked around to the front entrance and found an enormous square bar dominating the room. At the far corner sat two deeply tanned young women. One was wearing a yellow summer dress cut low, just barely keeping her breasts in check. Her companion was in a tube top and very brief orange shorts. Hughes guided Angie to two stools away from them. Angie eyed the two women and rolled her eyes at Hughes. "Even a non-detective can figure out why we're sitting here," she said. Hughes grinned.

After a minute, a bartender with a practiced short stubble and wavy hair pulled back into a ponytail approached. He smiled at Angie and said, "Welcome. I'm Randy. How can I serve you?"

Angie smiled back and said, "I think I'll have a Patron margarita."

"You bet," he replied, pausing before he turned to Hughes indifferently. "And you, sir?"

"Same." Hughes watched him move away with a slight urban roll.

"Jesus," Hughes said. "I thought he was going to come to you over the bar."

"When you've got it, you've got it. Let me try the photo this time."

"As long as you don't take him home to show it to him."

"Already got the best take-home guy."

"OK. Here's the photo," Hughes said as he watched Randy make the two drinks. He came back, one drink in each hand, placing Angie's down first. He smiled at her, then placed down Hughes's.

"Thanks," said Angie, looking up into his eyes. "Randy, could you do me a favor?"

He stopped in his tracks. "You bet. What can I do for you?" Sexuality oozed from his look like warm maple syrup.

"I'm looking for a cousin who I think is living here on the Shore. We don't get here often, so I'd like to look him up."

"Sure," he replied, now unsure. "What's his name?"

"I've got his picture here. Maybe you've seen him here?" she said, placing Arnold's photo on the bar, trying to keep it dry.

Randy looked at her, shrugged, then looked at the photo. "Nope, haven't seen him. Why do you think he was here?"

Angie gave him a disappointed look that had an effect. "I don't know, except we think he goes to a lot of clubs here on the Shore."

Randy glanced at Hughes, now a little suspicious. "This

is more of a family place with a lot of couples. You may want to try around Asbury Park. That's got a hot club scene."

"Gee, OK," Angie replied, switching from vamp to coquettish. "Any ideas of ones to try?"

"You may check out the Wonder Bar or Stone Pony. The Pony is where Springsteen got his start. When it's open, it gets a good crowd." He eyed Hughes. "Let me know if there is anything else I can help you with," he said as he moved down the bar and leaned over to the two women at the end.

"Well, at least we didn't get into a fight," she said. "Let's head down to Asbury Park. Nothing to lose."

"OK, super sleuth. We'll move on after these terrific margaritas."

They sat and sipped their drinks, watching the beachgoers file in. The place had a feeling of joie de vivre, like the atmosphere of an après-ski bar.

"I think I could really get into this area," Hughes said. Angie nodded back.

The bar and restaurant filled up with a preponderance of families and couples.

"I think your boyfriend, Randy, is right," Hughes said. "I don't think this is where we would find our subject."

"Some boyfriend," Angie replied. "He hasn't even suggested another Patron. I think you scared him off."

"Or you're more than he can handle." Hughes finished his drink and left his money on the bar. He gave her a soft pat on her bottom and said, "OK, let's head out to wilder hunting grounds."

Chapter 17

The night became fully dark as they left Jimmy's, the lights from the street lamps and beach houses giving off spotty glows.

With the top down on the Mustang, Hughes headed south with the ocean wall on their left. Angie clamped her cap back on and settled into the leather seat. Hughes put his left arm out and cruised slowly after being warned by Annie that the road was heavily patrolled by police looking for drunk drivers and speeders. The beach houses on the right side of the road were of varied design, giving a slight helter-skelter look. They passed fewer beach bars than Hughes thought there would be.

Thirty minutes later, they rolled into Asbury Park. It was a town that had seen high times, then inexplicably was ground down with drugs and a criminal element to become a beachfront slum. It was pulling itself back up like an out-of-shape contender, so there were pockets of revitalization in close proximity to boarded-up crack houses and crumbling shacks. But the signs of the revival were sticking out like fresh makeup on a tired but pretty girl.

Hughes could see activity on the boardwalk and people

on the street. A police car was blatantly parked on the street, a single officer slouched down behind the wheel. Hughes drove through what appeared to be the center of action and immediately spotted the Wonder Bar and then The Stone Pony. He continued along the beach road, then made a wide turn back, parking in a dirt lot near the Wonder Bar, which sat low in the sand under a large marquis advertising that night's band: The Nipple Kings. They sat silently in the car for a minute. Then Hughes said, "What do you think?"

"Well, I guess nothing ventured, nothing gained," Angie replied, pushing her door open.

"Wait," Hughes said. "Let strategize this. I'll go in first, and if I don't come back after a couple of minutes, join me at the bar. It will make sense that I check things out first."

"Why don't I go in first?" Angie said.

"Because you're the girl."

"Watch it, buster. This girl has moves you've never seen."

Hughes grinned at her. "I have to see if the guys who attacked me are around. We can go in together, but be ready to exit fast."

"I've got your back."

Still early, the Wonder Bar was only about half-filled. It smelled of sawdust and urine.

The bar was populated with males; three or four of them looked like they had been there for hours. Hughes paused as they entered, then nodded to Angie and headed to the bar. They slid onto two beat-up barstools and scanned the room. There was a small stage to one side and a guy with purple-dyed hair was tinkering with the audio mics. The low ceiling gave a closed-in feeling.

Eyeing the heavily tattooed woman tending bar at the

other end, Angie leaned over to Hughes and whispered, "Let me have the photo. We sisters stick together."

"If that's your sister, I'm dumping you."

After a couple of minutes, the bartender sauntered over, clearly in no hurry. She wore a tee shirt that said, "Heat and serve." "Life sucks, then you die" was tattooed on her left arm, and the Harley Davidson logo was on her right. She stopped in front of them, a wet rag in her hand. There were dark circles under her eyes and garish lipstick caked on her lips. She stared empty-eyed at Angie, ignoring Hughes.

Angie paused a minute, sizing her up, then said, "Love your tats. Beats the stupid rose I put on my left tit." The bartender smiled.

Ignoring Hughes, Angie said, "Patron shooter. Can't get through the night without it."

Hughes ordered a Bud Light. It was not acknowledged but arrived a minute later. A shot glass was put in front of Angie, and the tequila then poured into it. A lime was placed next to it on the bar.

Angie stretched her arms back, giving an appearance of boredom but having the added effect of bringing her breasts up nice and high. "What time does it wake up here?" she asked.

"By the way, my name is Rachel."

The bartender lingered and replied, "I'm Torrid; pleased to meet you. Not until around midnight."

"Torrid? That's cool," replied Angie. "I tend bar in a small club on Long Island. Fucking sick of getting hit on. You too?"

"Better believe it, but I bet you get better offers than I do. The creeps in here just want to go behind the dumpster. Can't figure out I'm not interested in them."

Hughes turned his back to the bar, seemingly ignoring them, scanning the room for any sign of Arnold.

"I hear you," Angie replied with an appropriate amount of disgust. She nodded toward Hughes and whispered, "I'm happy to be here on his nickel, but it does get old."

"I hear you, girlfriend. Be back, got a customer." She waddled to the far end of the bar.

Hughes watched her go, then said, "You going to invite her back for a party?"

"She'd kill you. Your eyes wouldn't uncross for a week."

"Yeah. Too much burning love for me. But it's you who would see a different side of her, not me."

"Whatever it takes."

Torrid came back, still holding the bar rag. Now she had a small smile and her eyes were not quite so empty. "So, what brings you to the Shore, girlfriend?"

Angie nodded again toward Hughes, who seemingly was not interested in their conversation.

"Heartthrob here has a boner for the nude beach. Works for me, too."

"We go there a lot. Maybe you would like to join us this weekend?" Torrid glanced around to see if there was anyone waiting for a drink. Satisfied not, she turned back to Angie. "You might have to leave numbnuts at home," she said, nodding toward Hughes.

Angie gave her a sultry smile. "That can probably be arranged. I can work on it."

Torrid gave her a look like a cat ready to eat a canary. "Another shooter? On me?"

"Sure. Night is young."

Torrid moved off to get the tequila. Hughes leaned over and mumbled, "Should I be jealous?"

"Sugar, you never know. But I'm doing this for you."

Torrid returned, the bottle in hand, and refilled the shot glass. She ignored Hughes.

Torrid leaned over the bar into Angie's space. Angie could feel her visual appraisal and the smell of cigarettes and sweat.

"Hey, I just remembered," Angie said. "I have a good girlfriend on Long Island who asked for a favor." She started searching her pockets, finally pulling out the photo of Arnold. "Her brother is supposedly roaming around somewhere down here. She said she's worried and asked to keep a lookout." She discreetly held up the photo. "Ever seen this dude?"

Torrid looked at the photo and shrugged. Then she said, "Yeah, I think I've seen him with a group of heavies. I think they hang around the Pony."

"Heavies, like in fat people?"

Torrid dropped her voice to a whisper. "No, girlfriend, heavies like in people you don't want to know."

"Shit," Angie said. "Kim won't be happy to hear that."

"You'll be a lot happier with the group on the beach. Maybe see another side. Tell your friend to forget that asshole brother of hers. No good will come if you mess with that group. This is the Jersey Shore, you know."

"I hear you, babes. How about I try to get back here alone in a day or two?" She glanced sideways at Hughes.

"Works for me," she said under her breath. She saw a couple of guys in leather vests with no shirts signaling to her. Glancing back to Angie, she said, "Got to get to work. Try to get back. Have some fun." She moved to the other side of the bar.

Angie looked over to Hughes and winked. "Pull me out of here like you mean it," she whispered.

Hughes took her by the arm and said loudly, "Let's get

out of here." He pulled her from the barstool, and they started out the door.

Torrid looked up from the other end as they left. Angie gave her a smile and a "what can I do?" look. Torrid mouthed, "Come back."

Outside, the night turned as sultry as a New Orleans summer. Many more people were around, giving the area a safer feel. Down the street was The Stone Pony. Young people in jeans and tee shirts could be seen going in. Hughes and Angie paused.

"Well, looks like you hit a home run. With me and her," he said to her. "It's unbelievable we were able to get a hit the first day together. Glad I brought you."

Angie grinned. "When you've got it, you've got it."

Looking across a dusty and littered empty lot, Hughes saw a sign for "Porta." Apparently, an Italian restaurant. "I'm hungry. Let's get a bite and figure out our next move."

"Better keep me fed and happy, buster. You saw how I'm in demand. And you need my detective moves."

"I need a lot of things with you. Let's head over there."

They went across and into Porta, a huge barn-like space with a large bar on the left and another smaller one across the room. It was busy and vibrating with the chatter of a crowd of pizza-eating half-drunks fortifying themselves for the night. Hughes and Angie seated themselves in the far corner of the bar and ordered two Coronas.

Hughes grinned at Angie. "Way to go, super sleuth. Of all the gin joints in all the world, you found out where our target is."

"Elementary, my dear shamus. It's called feminine guile."

"Now we have to figure out our game plan." Hughes

looked around at the cavernous room and saw nothing of concern.

"What are you thinking?" Angie asked.

Hughes took a sip of his beer and was quiet for a minute. "I'm thinking of going slow. The two gorillas jumped me for just showing a picture of Levine. Obviously, he's into something heavy and something we don't know about. See if you can do this. Strictly voluntary. Maybe you can go into The Stone Pony first and check things out. I saw a bunch of single women going in, so I don't think it would be unusual for a girl to go alone. Scope things out. If you see Levine, see who he's with, what he's doing. Don't show the picture, but maybe you can ask if they've seen a guy like him. If there's nothing for us, let me know, and I'll come in and we can hang out for a while to see if he's spotted. We have to be careful. I've learned to be patient."

"Yeah, like you have patience. But I get it. Let me scope things out first. Then we can figure it out."

"You've got it. Let's get a pizza for strength. By the way, be careful with the booze."

Angie grinned. Her eyes sparkled with the adventure. Hughes was worried she was too into it. Years kicking around in his business told him to be cautious. Too many possible surprises around the corner.

The bartender finally drifted over. She was impossibly young and perky with a smile that looked impossibly sincere. "Ready, guys?" she said.

"Yep," Hughes replied. "Let me ask you. Do you ever go to The Stone Pony?"

"Sure, when there's somebody playing there that I like."

"What's it like?"

"Like? Do you mean who goes there?" She leaned over the bar to them, glad to play tour guide. "Well, it's only open when there's a band playing there. It's a famous place. A lot of great rockers got started there."

"What's the crowd like?" Hughes was trying to play the eager tourist.

"All kinds. Sometimes come rough trade, depending on who's playing there. Like tonight, there's a punk band, so there will be some druggies and people you never see in the daylight."

Angie laughed. "You mean like vampires?"

"Pretty close. If you go there tonight," she said, eyeing them up and down, "be careful."

They ordered a margherita pizza and split a Caesar salad. They ate quietly, each thinking about what was coming up.

Porta echoed like a canyon. When they finished, Hughes left cash on the bar and they went out to the Mustang and sat for a while.

"OK," Hughes finally said. "Go in and do a walk-through. Use your excellent instincts. Look for our guy. Don't show the photo unless you can smooch a bartender with your 'we are all sisters' routine. Text me 'OK' if you think it is. I'll come in. 'No' if not. If it's a no, come right out."

Heavy clouds had moved in over the beach from the ocean side. Dark on top, they reflected the lights from the boardwalk, giving the bottom a strange pink glow. The humidity came up, giving a sultry and tropical feeling. An occasional female scream could be heard, either in panic or joy. Crowds were growing with the summer rites of pleasure.

Angie sighed and tugged on her tee shirt. Hughes wondered how he found a woman so beautiful, exciting, and so fearless. "Be careful," he said in a whisper as she got out of the car and then headed across the wide street. He watched her queue up at the entrance, apparently flirting with the doorman, and disappear into the club. He sat watching the street traffic and tuned in the radio to a rock station. Appropriate.

The next twenty-five minutes felt like two hours. A police officer cruised by and gave him a look, apparently decided he was no threat, and moved on. Finally, he saw Angie come out. She stopped at the entrance and gave some sexy body language, hand on hip, to the doorman, then started walking toward the car. Opening the car door, she was as excited as a kid on Christmas morning.

"He's in there," she breathed. "Honest to God. I saw the little shit. By the way, he looks like shit."

"You sure?" Hughes was in mild shock.

"Sure. He's with some really creepy people. Maybe some of the guys who jumped you."

"Unbelievable! We're lucky and good. How many people are there with him?"

Angie had trouble getting her breath. She watched as a Corvette rumbled past, her eyes as large as inkwells. "I think there are about four people altogether, including him. But it's hard to tell because everyone is moving around, getting ready for the band."

"Jesus." Hughes stared out the car window at the passing foot traffic. The clouds parted and a glowing half-moon hung over the water. He thought silently as Angie waited and looked at him. "Got to figure how to snatch him. I don't think he will just come along if we ask."

"By the looks of those goons with him, it will take a small army to snatch him."

"Any idea how many or who they could be?"

"Hard to tell, but they make the Sopranos look like Boy Scouts." Angie was still excited.

"If we stake out the parking lot and find what car they have, I can run the plates and maybe see who we are dealing with."

Angie stayed quiet. Then she said, "I could go back in and see if I could learn something. One in the group is the perfect Jersey bimbo."

"Which you are not. What makes you think they will accept you? Not to mention, it may be slightly dangerous."

She thought for a minute. "I could say a guy stood me up. Say I came from New York and met him on the beach. Maybe even say he was going to score me some blow, but he's not showing up. Maybe the girl will relate to that. By the looks of her, she's got experience in getting stood up."

"Darling, you've got some set of balls."

"Please. That's your department. All I've got is balls by association."

"OK. If you feel comfortable giving that a try, go back in. Anything we learn is a plus. Finding a solution is figuring out the problem. I'll get into a good surveillance spot and wait. Hit me with a generic text after about 20 minutes so I know you're OK."

Angie grinned. "This is more fun than sex. I think my name is Rachel. Do I look like a Rachel?"

"You look like an angel."

She smiled seductively. "OK, here I go. Undercover investigator Rachel on the job!"

She hopped out of the car and Hughes watched her head back to The Stone Pony, an attractive roll in the back of her pants. He waited a minute, then satisfied no one was paying any attention, started the Mustang and pulled to a spot where he could clearly watch the exit.

Chapter 18

Inside the club, the night was heating up. Outside, at the open-air stage, a skinny guy in cut-off jeans and a torn tee shirt was doing sound checks on the mic. Occasional band members wandered in from the back of the stage and watched the crowd filter in. A sign was stuck up next to the stage advertising the name of the band, Death Spiral. The indifference of the crowd was evident. The air in the entertainment area thickened and felt close, despite the open sky above.

At the inside bar, Musa, Tiffany, and Arnold were joined by two of Musa's friends, Luca and Tommy. Luca was short and thick with bulging arms stretching a Globe Gym tee shirt. His nose was crooked from a poorly fixed break years ago, making his face look off-center. His head was shaved and tanned. Tommy was young and lanky. His eyes seemed to sag down above a long, narrow face that, despite his age, gave him a sinister look. They both grinned at Musa, leaving no doubt as to who was the leader.

Tiffany already had downed two shots of tequila, and it showed. Her breasts bobbed like two soccer balls under her tee shirt that said, "Tequila makes my clothes fall off."

She laughed at practically everything Musa said. Arnold was grinning foolishly, his eyes vacant and wet. The bar in front of the group was littered with half-empty bottles and glasses. Other customers gave them room.

Musa smiled at Tiffany. "Off to another Jersey night, darling? Better pace yourself." He looked over at Arnold, who was standing unsteadily to Tiffany's right. "Need you to keep an eye on our good pal here. Maybe even get him laid."

Tiffany looked over at Arnold and made a face. "Good luck with that. Any babe fucking him will get stoned just by being near him." Then she laughed and said, "Getting any babe near him would have to be stoned, right Arnie?"

"Cut it out, Tiffany," Musa hissed. "Arnie needs to be happy." He leaned over Tiffany and slid a half-filled shot glass across the bar toward him. "Arnie, you're one of us. Don't let Tiffany give you any shit. She really loves you, and I do, too."

Arnold made a weak smile. "Yeah, I want to be happy." He picked up the shot glass and downed the contents in a gulp. He reeled slightly.

Luca leaned close to Musa. "Got anything for me?" he asked. Musa looked at him like he had just seen a snake on his dinner plate.

"We don't do business at the bar, asshole. See me in the can in about ten minutes."

Tiffany started moving to the music flowing into the bar. She put her arm around Arnold and pulled him close to her. "Oh, baby, you're sweaty. We have to clean you up a little before I introduce you to my girlfriends." She giggled.

Arnold smiled at her. "I could use a girlfriend. Bobby promised me more fun. Maybe I'll just go back to Boston."

Musa heard him and took Tiffany by the arm. "I told you to make him happy. He doesn't sound like it. Maybe you should give him a blow job later to help morale."

"Ugh," she replied. "But who knows? Buy me another tequila, Bobby. The night is young."

Arnold smiled at her. "I like that. You promised, Bobby."

"Count on me, Arnie. There is more pussy in here than you can handle. Right, Tiffany?"

Tiffany made a face at him, her back to Arnold.

People drifted by, many nodding or giving Musa a "hi" sign. Two women in their early twenties stopped. One was tall and gangly with black hair with purple highlights and bright-red lipstick. The other was shorter, well stacked but with unfortunate hips and thighs. Both were in white shorts and tube tops.

"Hi Elise," Musa said to the shorter girl. "Missed you on the beach the other day."

She smiled up at Musa, her face perfectly shaped, but her mouth slightly too wide. "Missed you, too. Forget the promise I made to you?" Elise oozed sexuality.

"Maybe tonight I'll collect. Stick around. I've got some business, then I'll be free to play."

Her eyes fluttered, and then she looked over at Arnold, who was staring at her with lust. She stepped back a bit, recognizing his heavy addiction. "Your friend looks like he's got a heavy package," she said coolly. "Is he with the group?"

"He's my package, so leave him alone unless you want to hook up."

Tiffany glared at the two women. "Let's have a round," she said and signaled to the bartender, making a drinks-all-around gesture.

The band started tuning up on the large stage in back. Tiffany took the taller woman by the hand and pulled her toward Arnold. "Marny, I want you to meet my friend, Arnold. He's visiting from Boston and helps make our parties go."

"Really," Marny replied warily. She recoiled slightly and glanced over to Elise, unsure.

"Yep. We can all party later, and you may find out Arnold's got some hidden talents."

Arnold grinned, showing off his yellowing teeth. Marny gave a slight shudder and gave Tiffany a look of disgust.

The drinks arrived and they all drank, toasting each other full of life on the Shore. The band started with a sound as explosive as a cherry bomb.

Chapter 19

A ngie was grim as she headed back to The Stone Pony. Despite the hot summer night, a shiver of cold fear ran down the middle of her back.

The entrance to The Stone Pony, with its simian doorman, loomed ahead like a yawning cave. She was trying to figure out what she would do aside from whining about being dumped by a guy. She decided that if her instincts sensed danger, she would say, "ladies room," and quietly disappear. Hughes would know what to do next.

The doorman, a hulk in a wife beater shirt and jeans remembered her, giving her a gap-toothed smile as she entered. Both his arms were heavily tattooed in confusing patterns, a testament to many nights of drinking.

As she stepped inside, the almost overwhelming stench of sweat and stale beer hit her like a wet sponge. In the forty minutes she was in the car with Hughes, the crowd had tripled in size and intensity. Now the bar was crowded and she couldn't see Arnold at first. She stood to the side, trying to get her bearings. Finally, she spotted him slouching against the bar in the middle of a scrum. She slowly made her way toward the group.

Standing near them, she tried to look as forlorn as

possible. After a couple of minutes, Tiffany looked over and spotted her. "Hey, babe," she called out. "Come over and join in. The more the merrier."

Angie gave her a wane smile. She shrugged and took a couple of steps toward the group. Bobby Musa glanced over and spotted her, appraising the way her breasts stretched out her tee shirt. His eyes rolled down her body, taking it all in. He nodded and eyed her like a mongoose sizing up a cobra. By this time, the group had grown to eight people, toasting each other for any perceived reason.

Tiffany reached out and took Angie's hand, pulling her into the group. "What's your name, honey? Where are your friends?" she said, also checking out Angie's body.

Angie took a deep breath, squeezed Tiffany's hand, and pulled hers away. "I'm supposed to meet a guy here, but I have a feeling the asshole stood me up."

Down the bar, a woman screamed and laughed loudly. It went unnoticed. Musa reached out and put his arm around Angie, his breath ripe with beer and lime. He said, "I think I'm the guy you're supposed to meet."

Tiffany gave him a hard look and pulled Angie toward her. "All guys are slime. So, what's your name?"

Angie glanced back at Musa, who was undressing her with his eyes. "I'm Rachel," she said. "I met this guy on the beach. We hit it off great, I thought. He was supposed to meet me here an hour ago and promised to take me out on his boat. But I haven't seen him since."

"Not a lot of guys with boats come into this place," Tiffany laughed. "We're much too earthy for them."

The temperature inside the Pony rose with the crowd. Angie grinned at the ongoing patter of the group she was standing with, trying to be a part of them. After the next round of drinks, Musa stepped over to her. He put his arm around her and said, "This is the way of the Shore; we're all one big family. We play together."

Angie let the pressure of his arm bring her slightly closer and smiled at him. "Wow, I guess so. You guys seem to be really alive."

Musa tried to understand that and thought for a minute, then said, "Stick with us. We will probably end up partying later at the house." He gazed lustily at her.

"Who?" she asked. "All of us here?"

"Sure. Maybe even more as the night goes on and more friends show up."

"I like the girls, especially Tiffany. Even that strange guy next to her in the ratty tee shirt."

Musa looked over at Arnold, who was trying to peer down Elise's tube top. "Yep, he's with us. Sort of our sugar daddy." He laughed at his joke.

The band launched into a modified version of *Brown Sugar* that made conversation nearly impossible. Musa leaned into Angie and yelled, "I will show you such a good time it will make your pussy sore."

Angie forced a smile. "Do all you guys live together?"

"Me and Arnie there stay in the house. Everyone else is welcome whenever they want to."

"Where's that?" Angie asked, trying to sound innocent.

"Close by." The sexual implication was almost clear.

Tiffany stepped over to them and took Angie's hand.

"Bobby, don't scare our new girl. Come over here, Rachel. We should do some girl talk," she said, pulling Angie away from Musa's arm. Angie took the opportunity.

"Thanks, Tiffany, for being so welcoming," she said, glancing over her shoulder at Musa, who apparently didn't want to challenge Tiffany.

"We're all fighting the same bastards," Tiffany replied

with a smile, glancing at Angie's stretched tee shirt. Angie felt Tiffany's vibe, feeling like the cream inside an Oreo cookie.

"What's with your friend there?" Angie asked, gesturing with a nod toward Arnold, who was leaning against the bar. Another guy, an obvious weightlifter, came into the group. His open shirt featured an enormous tanned chest. His jeans had a large steel chain hanging from one of the belt loops. Musa was distracted by him.

"Arnie, oh, he's Bobby's piggy bank. We have him hanging around because he supplies the bread. We just keep him happy."

"He looks stoned. Is he all right?" Angie made a face.

Tiffany giggled. "He is stoned. We keep him that way as part of the 'happiness' work. An occasional BJ from some babe works also."

"Jesus," Angie replied. "Don't look at me."

"You don't have to worry about that. Maybe worry about Bobby. But stick with me. Us girls should stick together."

Luca was in the process of ordering another round of tequila shots from the unhappy bartender. Tiffany told him to add one for Angie. The band started in outside on the stage with a crescendo of electric guitars, which raised the noise level even higher. A glass broke somewhere. Musa moved closer, bumping Angie's breast with his elbow.

"Where you from, honey?" Tiffany asked.

"Hempstead," Angie replied, allowing Musa another bump. "Here for a couple of days with my girlfriend. But she got sick and went home. I thought I would stay another day or so to relax on the beach. The guy I met seemed nice, but looks like he was bullshitting me."

"Happens," Tiffany said. "But you can hang with us. We take in everyone."

The drinks arrived, and the group loudly threw them back, toasting glory days.

Outside, two blocks away, Hughes slouched worriedly in the Mustang, trying to figure out the next move but was coming up blank. It's like he sent Angie out into the lion's den and just had to wait. To pass the time, he took out a small notepad and started listing case facts.

Chapter 20

The air in The Stone Pony continued to steam up and the crowd at the bar grew, even with the comings and goings of hangers-on. Musa started pushing for a party at his house. Angie eyed Arnold, who acted like an *Alice in Wonderland* character. It was evident he was under Musa's control.

When the next round of shots showed up, Angie told Tiffany she had to go to the ladies room, hoping she wouldn't want to go with her. Angie timed it just as Tiffany was collared by a scraggly, bearded biker who was infatuated with her ample chest. Angie quickly made for the ladies room and found it crowded with women standing in line for booths, preening in the mirrors, and discussing what they thought was the male talent in the club.

When the two women in front of her finally finished and opened the booth to her, she entered, locking the door behind her. She dropped her shorts to her ankles and sat down, pulling out her cell phone. A fast text to Hughes told him she was planning to go to the house to see where it was and for him to watch for them after she sent a "go" message. She had just finished when Tiffany banged on the door to the booth with urgency. "You in there, Rachel?" she yelled. "We're getting out of here pretty soon. Bobby's anxious."

"Here I come," Angie yelled back, flushing.

Outside, Hughes started the car and pulled to the corner where he could watch the front door, hoping to be able to spot Angie as she left. He waited, sinking low in the front seat, deep in the shadows from the streetlights. Forty-five minutes later, his phone alarmed a text coming in. It said "go" in capital letters.

Minutes later, a loud crowd emerged. Hughes thought in the group was one of the guys who had attacked him a week earlier. He also saw four women, one obviously very drunk, and the raven hair and erect posture of Angie. He gave them a hundred-yard head start, then got out of the car and followed.

The air smelled of low tide and a thick dew was settling in. It was an easy tail, the group laughing and yelling obscenities. Past a junk-littered empty lot, they moved to a row of tired wooden houses, finally pouring into one with dim lights on inside. Hughes watched them from a distance. He saw Angie with them and ran back to the car. He drove up and parked a half-block away in the shadows.

Inside, the party was taking off. Tiffany decided to do an impromptu dance, working to get some parts of her shaking and jiggling. Musa poured a pile of cocaine on the coffee table, offering it to one and all. Arnold sat in a tattered armchair, apparently asleep. Angie stood to one side, trying to figure an out. After several minutes, Musa sidled over to her and, leaning one arm against the wall, pinned her with his body. Angie could smell the lust in his breath.

"How about you and me getting better acquainted?" he said, breathing heavily.

"Gee, Bobby, I hardly know you," she laughed back to him. She tried to slide to her left.

"Come, babe. You'll love it."

"Let's meet up tomorrow in a spot a little more romantic," Angie tried feebly, getting very scared.

"Nah. This place is as good as any." Musa leaned more into her, his chest through his open shirt pressing into her breasts. His other hand reached down and pushed hard between her legs.

"Nice bush. I like that," he panted. From across the room, Tiffany yelled at him. He turned to look at her.

"How about another drink first?" Angie said, slight desperation in her voice.

Musa thought for a minute, weaving. "Yeah," he said. "I can always use another drink." He pulled away, releasing her.

Angie smiled up at him. "Got more tequila?" She stepped to the side.

Musa grinned and turned back to the room. A couple was entwined on the couch across the room. "Stay right here," he muttered, heading to the kitchen for another bottle.

"Just a quick stop at the ladies room," she said with a wink.

"OK, be right back. A couple of shooters and we can party. No one comes to Bobby Musa's place without paying her dues," he said over his shoulder.

Angie quickly went into the bathroom down the short hall. When she entered the bathroom, the smell hit her like rotten fish. She tried the lock on the door and found it didn't work. Frantic, she pulled her shorts down, sat, and took out her cell phone. A text to Hughes went out: "Danny, close to getting raped. What can I do?"

Outside in the Mustang, Hughes heard the chirp of the text coming in. As he read it, a cold shiver went down his back. He thought, then replied, "Throw up on him and try to get out. I'm down the street on the left. GET OUT OF THERE!"

Musa opened the door just as she was putting her phone back in her pocket. "Hurry up, babe. I'm ready for you." He grabbed his crotch obscenely. Angie stood, quickly pulling up her pants, and gave him a wane smile. "Right behind you. Let's get those drinks," she said.

Musa took her by her arm and pulled her into the living room. The couple on the couch was now engaged in full sex, ignored by the rest of the group. Musa had lined up four shot glasses, each filled to the brim with amber tequila. He picked up one and handed it to Angie. He picked up another and threw it back. "Your turn," he said.

Angie smiled and drank it. She tried to get going a gag reflex. The two other shot glasses were picked up by Musa, one in each hand. Harsh music screamed in the room. He handed one to Angie, shook his head like a horse at an oasis and downed one of them. Angie summoned up serious "ill power," threw the drink into her mouth and, choking, vomited it back out onto Musa's open shirt and chest.

"Fuck!" he screamed. "What the fuck?" He looked down at the slop on his front. "You bitch!"

"Oh my God," Angie yelled. "I'm so sorry."

Musa snarled, turned, and made for the kitchen. Angie turned around and walked quickly to the front door, wiping her mouth with her arm. No one paid attention to her. On the porch, the fresh air hit her like escape.

Stumbling down the front steps, she saw the Mustang close by. Over her shoulder, she saw no one come outside and made for the car. Hughes opened the passenger door for her and she dove inside.

"Lie down," he said as he put the car into gear, driving slowly. He was just past the house, with Angie lying on the floor, when he looked in the side mirror and saw a large man come outside, looking around. Seconds later, he turned the corner and accelerated away.

"Jesus. God. Shit!" Angie murmured as Hughes sped away from Asbury Park. The lights from the dashboard made her pale face even more so. "What a bunch of sicko perverts," she said, shaking her head, trying to sober up.

"You had me scared to death," Hughes said, driving the speed limit but with a constant eye in the rearview mirror. "I had to be out of my mind to let you go in there. I'm usually the one who's said to have more balls than brains."

Settling down, Angie said, "Well, at least we found the lost Arnold Levine."

Thick fog was rolling in off the ocean, and headlights glowed like eyes in a backlit jack-o'-lantern.

"Just take it easy. We'll get back to Red Bank and clear our heads. Figure out what to do next."

Angie nodded.

The ride back to the Molly Pitcher was uneventful. The inn was lit like a birthday cake when they got back. Hughes parked the car in back, just in case, and they strode through the lobby. Ginger Christmas was on duty at the desk and smiled as they came through.

"How about a nightcap?" Hughes asked. Angie swallowed back the taste of the tequila and said maybe something weak would be OK.

They walked into the dark bar. The dark wood paneling

made the bar feel cavernous, which was in stark contrast to the otherwise bright feel of the inn. They found a table in a far corner, sat, and sighed. Angie made a weak smile. Hughes returned it with a grimace.

A couple of minutes later, a well-preserved waitress in a white blouse and black skirt came to the table and greeted them, obviously picking up on their stress. Hughes ordered a Jameson on the rocks and Angie, a cappuccino. They were quiet waiting for the drinks. When they arrived, the waitress courteously moved away and left them alone.

Hughes took a sip and tried to smile. "Close one. My fault for letting you go in there."

Angie shook her head. "No, it was my call. Got out of there and learned a lot."

"What? That the group we are dealing with are a bunch of lowlifes?"

None of the three customers in the bar were paying any attention to them, and they slowly relaxed.

"No," she said. "We know where our guy is and what has happened to him. Dan, he's like a zombie. I think they have drugged the shit out of him. I think they are using him as a piggy bank, keeping him stoned, and tapping his trust fund."

"And, obviously, the people doing this are bad people."

"So, mister big-time private eye, what do we do about this?" Angie sipped her cappuccino as the color returned to her face.

"He's of age, so we can't call this a kidnapping. I don't think we can prove any criminal actions, so I think the cops are out. We are going to have to do a grab and hopefully get him into rehab. What is obvious, we can't do this ourselves. We need some help. Tomorrow, we check out and head home while I figure this out."

"Some vacation. You sure know how to show a girl a good time."

Hughes smiled at her. He left payment on the table, and they headed to their room, suddenly exhausted. They slept fitfully, Angie finally spooning into Hughes and holding him close.

Chapter 21

Early the next morning, sunlight poured into the room like a golden blanket. They woke together. Angie headed into the shower without a word, while Hughes sat at the maple desk and made notes. They learned a lot and were unbelievably lucky.

Angie came out wrapped in an oversized white towel, her hair wet and glistening. "I feel human again," she said. "Washed the filth from last night."

Hughes was quiet as he looked at her and was taken again by her natural beauty. "We have to go back home," he said. "Need help with this, I think. Need to talk to our clients and figure this situation out. It's a lot more than a simple locate."

"Can't wait to get back," she replied. "The Jersey Shore feels sick and dirty to me. I know that's not fair, but I'm creeped out from last night."

"There are bad people everywhere. Certainly, Jersey's got its share. Let's finish this case and then think about coming back under better circumstances." He picked up the phone and ordered two full breakfasts from room service. "Let's pull ourselves together and get back on the road. We can think about this in the car."

Thirty minutes later, room service was served by a fresh-faced and handsome waiter who could have come out of Central Casting for a fraternity movie. They ate silently in front of the large window, watching boaters slowly cruise out of the river, leaving finger ripples behind them.

Angie waited as Hughes checked out, and they carried their luggage around back to where the car was hidden. Minutes later, they were on the Garden State Parkway, heading north. Hughes called the Levines from the car, making an appointment for the following morning. He didn't give any details, except to say progress was being made and it was important they discuss.

There was only a slight delay at the George Washington Bridge. They picked up the Saw Mill River Parkway at full speed and were on the Merritt soon afterward. Angie settled into the leather seat, quietly watching the passing scenery, lost in her thoughts. As they entered Boston, she finally brought up the night before.

"Danny, although last night was horrifying and scary, I have to admit, it was pretty exciting."

"You know," Hughes replied, "every time I think I'm fed up with the struggle to make money and getting clients, I think about how much I love getting up every day and doing what I do. I'm never bored and each day is an adventure. How many people can say that?"

"You just have to keep your head screwed on right, bumping into lowlifes all the time."

"Need to approach it with a sense of humor—the follies of human beings."

"Yep, but good to be home," Angie whispered.

The powerful car ran through the Prudential Tunnel and into Back Bay. After two laps around Beacon Hill,

Hughes put the car into the Boston Common Garage, and they hiked up the hill to Joy Street. For no reason they could think of, both felt exhausted.

The suitcases remained filled as they headed down to Charles Street for dinner. The bar at Toscano was beautifully appointed with a vague modern Italian feel and was empty at the early dinner hour. They sat at the corner of the bar with Tony the bartender greeting them by name. They ordered and shared a caprese salad and penne with meat sauce, having a glass of Chianti each. They walked back up the hill on Chestnut Street and around to Joy Street, which further tired them and capped the day and trip.

Hughes left the windows open and they crawled into cool sheets. The sounds of the street provided white noise. During the night, a fresh breeze blew in from the west and, with it, clouds heavy and dark with moisture. The rain started shortly after midnight. The sound settled into the deep consciousness of Hughes's mind, bringing relaxation. He half-woke and listened to the patter of rain on the windowsill and sidewalk outside, forgetting for a while about the Jersey Shore.

Early the next morning, Hughes woke to a full, heavy summer rain with a low pewter ceiling of clouds stretching over the city. Angie was brewing coffee and dressing in spurts.

He padded to the bathroom, surprised at how refreshed he felt. It was now "game on" for the Levine case. Finishing his morning ritual, he sat at his office desk and thought while the coffee was percolating.

His life seemed to be always in a spinning wheel, racing from one issue to another. He realized long ago he was not going to get rich being a PI. The life was certainly exciting, never the same, always different. But it seemed like he was always the voyeur, never part of the party. Always suspicious. Always cynical. Always bemused.

The delicious smell of fresh coffee headed his way and broke his thoughts. Probably a good thing.

"Morning, sunshine," Angie called. "The coffee fairy is on the job. Ready?"

"You bet," he whispered. "I'm going to see the Levines this morning to discuss the situation. Then I'm calling Ralph Lampley to see if he's available."

"Jesus, getting out the big guns, are we?" Angie remembered Ralph from when he helped Hughes in a tough surveillance case before. Ralph's scary exterior hid his inner sense of humor and quiet competence. With his tree-trunk arms and thick chest, Ralph was the person Hughes said he would always want to have his back. His loyalty to Hughes was obvious.

"Need help with this if the Levines still want to go forward. Personally, I think Arnold is a lost cause and they should write him off. We'll see."

Angie brought a cup of steaming black coffee to him as he sat at his desk. She was in a bra and black skirt. He grinned at her as he accepted the coffee. She grinned back at him, shaking her head.

Dressed in a black tee under a tan summer sports coat and khaki slacks, Hughes headed into the rain, a large blue umbrella his only defense. He headed down Beacon Street, dodging only a few people hurrying up the sidewalk to the statehouse atop the hill. Cutting around the Public Garden, he headed down Marlboro Street. The thick tree leaves gave some shelter, but every crosswalk was a small river he had to jump over. By the time he reached the Levines' townhouse, his feet were soaked and his jacket, limp. Ira greeted him with an "oh, my" as he opened the heavy oak door.

"Come in. Come in," he muttered. "You look soaked. Put your umbrella over there," he said, indicating a corner of the foyer. "I'll call Sara. She is anxious to hear what you've discovered."

Hughes followed Ira up the stairs to the musty living room. Sara Levine was seated in her overstuffed chair, eyeing him with contempt, a demon god you might find in a Buddhist temple. The dress she was wearing could have qualified as a paisley car cover.

"Well, Mr. Hughes, what have I gotten for my money?" she said caustically. Hughes waited for an invitation to sit and, getting none, sat opposite her on a frayed bench. He waited to see if Ira sat down, and when he didn't, he gave Sara a half-smile and started his briefing.

"In my business, you have to be lucky as well as good," he started. "With some of both, we were able to locate Arnold."

Ira and Sara looked at each other.

"We believe he is under the influence of some bad people who are using drugs to control him. If money is disappearing, it is because they've convinced him to give it to them."

Sara looked disgusted. She rolled her eyes at Ira, then turned back to Hughes. "You were supposed to find Arnold and bring him back. You are not doing your job."

"Mrs. Levine," Hughes replied, a hint of sarcasm in his voice. "We did what you asked. Found Arnold. I don't know of any other investigator who could have done it. By doing so, I got attacked by two strangers and had to get my assistant involved. By law, Arnold is capable of making his own decisions. We can verify that he is not being held completely against his will. I doubt he will come back voluntarily if we simply ask him to do so. If you want, I will give you his address and you can ask him yourself. In the meantime, here is an invoice for services rendered." He stood up.

Ira, suddenly panicked, said, "Mr. Hughes, we appreciate what you've done and we need your help." Turning to Sara, he said, "Don't we, dear?" After a minute, she nodded. Hughes sat back down.

"What do you recommend, Mr. Hughes?" she said. Only the faraway sound of rain pouring onto the street could be heard.

"I'll need help. You have to authorize it, and it may be expensive."

"Go on."

"If we can get our hands on Arnold and get him into rehab, there is a chance he can be straightened out. In any event, he must get away from the people he's with. That's a tall order. We can't be involved in a kidnapping situation, and the people we would be dealing with are not nice people. But if we can get him alone, maybe we can accomplish that. Not easy, and you should understand it is not a slam dunk."

"Slam dunk?" said Ira, clearly confused.

"I mean, it's a long shot."

Sara considered Ira as though he should simply play with his marbles. With a loud sigh, she said to Hughes, "OK, Mr. Hughes. Do what you must. We want Arnold back here. But if that's not possible, we at least want the money to stop disappearing."

Hughes stood again. "Wire me an advance for expenses; the instructions are on the invoice. I'll stay in touch and let you know how it's going."

Ira said he would get the umbrella as he led Hughes down to the door. When he opened it, water splashed inside. He stepped back, saying, "Thank you. I know you will do your best." He gave a half-smile as Hughes stepped into a tropical Marlboro Street.

Chapter 22

In Asbury Park, the all-night rain had stopped, leaving the morning in the village steamy and empty of tourists. Musa was sprawled across a foul-smelling bed upstairs. He was alone in the sparsely furnished room. Downstairs, Arnold Levine stood at the front window, staring out.

An overweight girl in a bra and panties walked across the room and into the kitchen. Her hair was frizzy and mousy-brown, and there was some black eye makeup smeared on her face. Arnold turned as he heard her open and close the refrigerator. She sat at the table and drank from a bottle of beer. He tried to remember the night before, but only had a vague recollection of people and sweat. "What's your name?" he asked the girl.

"I'm Sheila. Don't you remember? Oh, you were pretty wasted." She stifled a burp.

"Sort of. I don't feel so well. Can I have some of your beer?"

"There's more in the fridge. Help yourself."

Arnold was looking in the refrigerator when Musa walked in. He was wearing a pair of cutoff jeans and scratching his stomach. He gave Sheila a sour look.

"I hope you made Arnie happy," he said. Sheila smiled back obscenely.

"OK," he said, reaching into his pocket and taking out some bills. Counting out one hundred dollars, he gave it to Sheila and said, "Now get out. We can meet again in the Pony. Get your clothes on."

Sheila took the money and got up without a word, wiggling her way back into the living room.

Arnold turned to Musa. "Some night, huh, Bobby?"

"Yeah, some night. Need some more cash if we continue to party." Musa took a beer from Arnold's hand and started drinking it himself.

Arnold paused. He turned and looked out the kitchen window to the backyard. There was a charcoal grill with the lid open surrounded by plastic chairs, one of which was tipped over on the ground. A rancid smell flowed in through the open kitchen window.

"I think we have to stop hitting the fund," Arnold said shakily. "My folks have got to know how much we are spending and they are sure to be pissed."

"Well, if we run out of money, I don't know how I can get my dealers to supply product." He opened the refrigerator and stared inside, finally pulling out a beer for himself. "Besides, it costs money to have a good time."

"I know," said Arnold. "But I kind of miss home. Sometimes it's just a blur here."

"That's because you're having such a good time," Musa explained without conviction. He was getting concerned about Arnold's attitude, wondering if his control was wearing off. "Nothing at the Pony tonight. Thought we could head over to the Wonder Bar for a few pops later on."

"Don't know if I want to," Arnold replied, taking his

beer and walking into the living room. Musa regarded him with a mixture of disgust and worry.

With the rain gone, the day warmed up like an electric heater, the temperature heading into the low nineties. Musa sat on the front porch while Arnold played a video game. He decided he had to boost morale to keep the piggy bank open. After a while, Tiffany called. "Babes, round up a couple of your girlfriends. I want to take everyone to Gunnison for the day."

She giggled her approval.

By one o'clock, they were squeezed into a van Musa borrowed from Tony Loproente. The cost of the van was Tony going with them to the nude beach. Tiffany brought along two of her friends, Kymmy and Janey, who both were still blurry-eyed from the night before. They drove up the coast, through the thick summer traffic, and into the state park. The parking lot was already almost totally full.

Piling out, the group off-loaded their gear, including two fat-tire carts, coolers, blankets, and chairs. It was a long, hot walk to the actual beach, where they found all areas near the water taken by territorial groups.

Finding a spot four rows deep, they spread out their gear. The three girls immediately pulled off their clothes and dashed into the water, splashing around like children. Musa planted himself in a beach chair, while Arnold fell asleep in the sand. It couldn't be determined if Arnold was happier or not. Musa was getting more worried.

Chapter 23

H ughes told Ralph he would meet him at four o'clock at 29 Newbury restaurant at an outdoor table. The rain had cleansed the city but left a stifling humidity. Trees in the Public Garden sagged as if exhausted by the summer. Twenty-nine Newbury was a smart little bistro with a regular clientele who hung around the bar a couple of steps below street level. The outdoor café was ringed with potted flowers and provided excellent people watching.

Hughes took a table in the corner and waited, watching the very chic women pass by. Angie was working and asked him to say hello to Ralph for her. He ordered a Samuel Adams Summer Ale.

Twenty minutes later, he noticed a woman glance over her shoulder and he guessed Ralph was on his way. He always attracted looks from women, openly interested. He looked down the street and, sure enough, Ralph was coming down from Berkeley Street. He was wearing black leather slacks and, stretched over a massive chest, a white tee shirt that said "Everlast." Despite his size, he seemed to float over the sidewalk. He grinned as he approached and saw Hughes smiling back at him. He glided into the table area and settled across from Hughes. A waitress, pretty and petite, approached immediately.

"I see who has the stuff," Hughes said. "I've been sitting here for twenty minutes and was ignored. You show up and a foxy waitress is standing next to the table."

"Man, when you got it, you got it." Ralph's voice was a velvet whisper.

"What can I get for you?" the waitress in a starched white blouse and tight black skirt asked huskily.

Ralph just smiled up at her. Finally, Hughes said, "Get him a Patron margarita. And I'll have another beer."

The waitress said to Ralph, "I'm Hanna. I'm here to serve you. Be back in a minute with the drinks." She hardly noticed Hughes. Ralph watched her go.

"OK, what's up, boss?" he finally asked. Ralph filled his chair, a presence as thick and serene as a Buddha in a temple.

"Well, big guy, I took a case that I thought was a simple locate. My clients have this son of dubious origins who took off. Turns out, he's a trust-fund kid with a bundle from his grandfather and they were watching him hit the fund at an alarming rate. They wanted me to find him and maybe get him to come home."

"So, what's the problem?"

The waitress, Hanna, arrived with the drinks, bending over nicely as she served them. She smiled at Ralph and wiggled away. A soft perfume from the row of flowers on the surrounding rails wafted across the table.

"It looked like the kid was running around the Jersey Shore, so off I go. When I start asking around, a couple of cretins start pushing me around. Seems like they are protecting something a lot more serious than a kid with more money than brains. After meeting again with the clients, I head back down, this time with Angie."

Ralph grinned. "Nice to mix pleasure with work."

"You know me, dedicated."

"By the way, how is the luscious Angie? The only reason I'm here is because of her, not your ugly face."

"Working. And I have to keep her away from the hounds—including big black guys like you with beer-barrel chests."

"OK, I guess I have to suffer." He paused. "So, you stuck your nose into something and got it moved around on your face for doing so."

"That's pretty accurate. So now I'm back with Angie and we find the guy. Pure luck. Angie gets close to him, and it looks like they've got the guy pretty much set up as a drug slave, using him to loot the fund."

Hanna came back and asked if everything was all right. She appraised Ralph without embarrassment.

Hughes shook his head and continued. "Because the kid's of age, I can't see anything blatantly illegal. But it's pretty obvious the kid is under their control. So I figure all we can do is snatch the kid and get him into rehab. When his head is screwed back on, let him decide if he wants to continue to support his capturers."

"So, who are these guys?" Ralph finished his drink and held his glass up to the waitress, who was standing by the restaurant entrance. She arrived back in an instant.

"They seem to be a combination of the Sopranos and a bunch of perverted ghouls. Angie just barely got away with her innocence intact."

"Yeah, her innocence. I love that kind of innocence. So, what's the plan?"

"I thought maybe you could reason the kid away from

the bad guys while I run interference. See if we can get him home and into rehab."

"What do you think the cops would have to say about that?" Ralph smiled at the waitress, who smiled back. He was distracted for a moment, then said, "I may be tied up later today."

"Pay attention," Hughes chided. "If we get the kid back, my client will pay dearly. Everyone is happy. By the looks of him, we may even save the kid's life. I plan to inform most of what we are doing to the cops ahead of time. If we get a good detective, they may even give us some unofficial help."

Ralph thought for a minute. "I like it," he said. "I hustle his hopelessly addicted ass back to Boston. He runs off again and then we do it all over again. The gift that keeps on giving."

"So jaded," Hughes said, glancing over to the waitress, who was looking at Ralph like he was a Thanksgiving dinner.

"When's this going to happen?"

"Very soon. I'm going to rent a nice big SUV and head back down. Angie's coming, too."

"Even better. I'm in." Then, "Just a minute." Ralph got up, went to the waitress, and whispered something to her. She stared back at him, then nodded. He came back to the table, grinning. "Can't go today," he said. "Busy for a while."

Hughes sighed. "OK, I'll call you tomorrow morning. Get ready to go."

He finished his beer and signaled for the check. While Ralph sat at the table, Hughes headed back toward Beacon Hill, smiling to himself. He was sweaty by the time he got back to his apartment. He changed into shorts and a new tee shirt with his favorite New Balance shoes and headed to LA Fitness for a workout. He had an hour or so before Angie finished her shift and, hopefully, popped in to say hello and get caught up on the plan.

LA Fitness was gleaming, state-of-the-art, all glass and chrome. Despite the blistering August afternoon, it was cool inside and, therefore, busy with affluent twentysomethings.

Chapter 24

The eye candy in the club was so exceptional, his usual hour-long workout continued for a pleasurable two hours. Hughes showered afterward, then headed back into the fading August dusk. The grass on the Common was wilting from the hot summer weather. Several couples languished on blankets; some embraced without inhibition. Hughes smiled to himself as he made his way up the hill to Joy Street. He was looking forward to seeing Angie. There was already a hint of the end-of-summer musk in the air.

As he climbed the steps to his second-floor apartment, he heard soft jazz from inside. Opening the door with his key, he found Angie sitting on the couch, a dewy glass of white wine in one hand, an open magazine in the other. She had taken off her bartender's outfit and was in cotton shorts and a light pullover top. Her feet were bare, with one foot keeping time to the music. "Hi, babes," she said, looking up. "Hot today. You look all sweaty."

"I was beautiful until I walked from the sports club to home."

"I have an excellent sauvignon blanc in the fridge that I

picked up on the way home. I got out a little early because business was so slow. I guess everyone's out of town."

"Well, we're still here, but pretty soon back to the Jersey Shore. I met with Ralph Lampley, and he's in for the case. Hopefully, I can keep him focused."

He went to the kitchen and found the wine, icy cold, in the refrigerator. After a brief search, he found a wine glass in the rear of the cupboard and did a healthy pour. He plopped on the chair opposite Angie, took a sip, and grinned at her. "How about Mistral tonight?"

Angie snorted. "Hey, big spender. Think just because you wine and dine in fancy places, I'll come across?"

"One can hope."

Angie paused and took a tiny sip of her wine. "Well, I've been known to succumb to the charms of a certain hunky PI, if he plays his cards right." She paused again. "What's the occasion?"

"Thought we could talk about the next trip on the 'Snatch the Levine' caper."

Angie looked thoughtful. "Yeah, I want to talk about it. I think you should back off this one. Too many unknowns and too many creeps. Do they owe you any money?"

"You mean the Levines? No, I got a decent advance. But I want to finish this. Their son is in a bad place with some bad people. I can help maybe save someone."

"How about saving yourself? There are a lot of bad people involved. I haven't forgotten the situation I had with the guy they call Bobby. Have you forgotten about getting roughed up just for asking about Levine?" Angie was sitting straight up and staring at Hughes.

"I know, Angie," Hughes half-mumbled. "But I made a commitment. More importantly, these people need someone to help them and their kid. Sometimes evil has to lose."

"A white knight? OK, I think we need to talk about this over a glass of wine. Let me shower and get ready. Mistral, huh? Maybe you're my white knight."

Angie hopped up and headed for the bathroom. Hughes poured himself another glass of wine and stood at the window. On Beacon Street, couples walked slowly up and down, giving into the heat.

He yelled to her, "Take your time. Let's let the day cool." He settled back onto the couch and thought to himself, listening to the soft jazz. The gentle beat relaxed him and let his mind flow.

Angie fussed in the bathroom for almost an hour. When she emerged, what makeup she had on was invisible. Her hair was pulled up and secured with a tie. She was wearing a white bra with a matching thong and headed into the bedroom. "One of these days, maybe I will totally move in here so I can have clothes to wear." After a couple of minutes, she came back into the living room, now wearing white Armani slacks and a black silk shirt. Hughes, once again, was stunned.

"OK," he said. "Guess I can't wear white slacks. I am totally upstaged. Let me figure out something that a big-time, big-deal private eye would wear and we can head out."

Dusk had passed and, along with it, the stifling heat. An eastern breeze off the harbor filtered in to make the evening all but perfect. They decided to walk to Columbus Avenue, enjoying the city lights in soft focus from a thin mist.

Across the Public Garden, flowers were losing their strength but still shared their fragrance with the evening strollers. They strolled down Boylston Street, then south on Clarendon, then right on Columbus to the shaded front door of the restaurant. Valets already had parked a Ferrari and a Bentley in front. Katie, a sweet Asian in a short black dress, smiled as they entered. "Good evening, Dan. Hi, Angie. Welcome back," she said, greeting them.

"It's nice to go where they know your name," Hughes chuckled. Angie gave Katie a hug and asked about the baby.

"You can see her grow," Katie said. "Going to the bar again?"

"Yep, we'll be at the corner," Hughes said as he looked at the crowded bar.

They made their way past the lounge filled with couples and pairs of women. Hughes could not stop staring at some of the summer dresses. The women were like colorful flowers in an Armani landscape, some only slightly dressed. Angie gave him a withering look as they sat in an open section at the corner of the bar. A gazelle-like bartender glided over immediately. She had striking blue eyes that almost took away from the low-cut dress she was wearing. Angie gave Hughes another look.

Hughes sighed, "Life is good." He ordered a Ketel One martini and Angie, an unoaked chardonnay. The drinks arrived promptly. The bartender, remembering them from before, simply ran a check and kept it on the back bar.

Taking a tiny sip from her wine glass, Angie looked into Hughes's eyes and quietly said, "Let's rethink this whole Levine thing. I have a bad feeling about it."

Hughes thought for a moment. "I do, too. But I gave my word I would help and I don't feel I can bail out now. Ralph Lampley will help."

"Yep, that helps. But the two of you can't take on the Jersey Mafia."

Couples drifted in and the restaurant filled, despite it being deep summer.

"Looks like not everyone is out of town," Hughes said.

"Don't change the subject. This case is very dangerous. I don't like it."

"I know, Angie. I won't blame you if you stay behind. Ralph and I can handle it."

She looked deep into his eyes. "There is no way I will not stay with you. But your sense of danger is way different from mine. Sometimes I don't think you have a sense of danger."

"I just don't fear dirtbags. That's what we have down on the Shore. They are tough in their minds in their own little turf. But not really. Ralph is tough, not those guys."

The bartender came back to them. "What's your first name?" Hughes asked.

"I'm Kimberly. Are you having dinner with us tonight?" Getting a nod from Hughes, she placed down two menus and set up place settings. Hughes ordered another martini. Angie glared at him.

He caught the look and said, "Two is the limit. I can handle it."

Angie shook her head.

They both ordered the tuna tartare and decided to share a Caesar salad and a margherita pizza. Kimberly took the order and smiled. Not tourists.

Angie continued to sip daintily at her wine; the food arrived shortly after. As they ate, Angie sighed and said, "OK, what's the plan?"

Hughes drank some of his drink, paused, then said, "OK, this is what I think we can do. You said Levine is pretty much a zombie. So, we wait until we see this, and Ralph puts his arms around him and puts him into the car. You drive. I will run interference."

"Interference with what, your good looks?"

"If I have to, I will reason with them."

"And how do you stay out of the morgue or jail?" Angie was getting curt.

"I plan to talk to the cops ahead of time. We are not kidnapping. If Levine refuses to go with us, we bail. No crimes will be committed. But if he is in a drug-induced state, we can say we are bringing him to rehab. Which is exactly what we are doing. The key is to get him away from the control freaks. If we can do that, we head back to Boston rapidly and deliver him to his parents. What he does next is up to him and them."

"This sounds very flawed. Where and how do you get him to get into the car?" Angie took a small piece of her salad and chewed it thoughtfully. Hughes put down his fork and picked up a slice of the pizza. The noise level in the restaurant rose to a jungle hum.

The general manager, Mark, looking perfect in a black Canali suit, came to welcome them. Hughes had helped in the past with a dishonest office worker who had found a way to print vendor checks to herself. Mark shook Hughes's hand and gave Angie a kiss on the cheek. As always, he had the room running as smoothly as a Rolex watch.

"Like I said, always good when they know your name," Hughes whispered with a chuckle when Mark continued into the dining room.

He continued their conversation. "I'm renting a large SUV. We pick up Ralph and head back down. But this time, it's not the plush and comfortable Molly Pitcher but an anonymous motel. I plan to talk to the cops before we do anything to try to stay out of jail. Then we 'reason' Arnold back to Boston and maybe even get him into some kind of rehab."

"That's it? That's your plan?" Angie took a larger sip of her wine and glanced around at the pretty people at the bar. She shook her head.

"Well, I admit it's a little thin, but simple is usually better. I just want to wrap this up as best as we can. With Ralph along, we will have a good foundation."

Angie just looked at him. She held up her glass for a refill to the stunning bartender. Hughes checked his martini glass and did the same. They were quiet for a while, taking small sips from their new drinks. The din of the room seemed to recede, with each in their own thoughts. Somehow they seemed closer to each other.

After a steamy night, Boston woke to a freshening breeze with the first hint of a change of season. The grass in the Common started to have a slight musty smell to it. Hughes made a couple of calls and secured a large black GMC SUV. He then placed a call to Ralph, letting the phone ring seven times before a female voice answered, "What?"

"Is Ralph there?" Hughes asked. There was background noise sounding like chairs scraping across a tile floor.

After a minute, "Whoever this is, your timing sucks."

"Ralph, it's Dan. We're getting ready to head south."

An angry female voice could be heard in the background. "Oh, yeah," Ralph said. "Call back in half an hour. I'll be with you, bro." He hung up.

Angie was folding some shorts for the trip. She looked over to Hughes and rolled her eyes. "I guess the plan is underway," she said with no effort to hide the sarcasm.

Hughes shrugged, then pulled out a leather duffel from the closet and threw in a couple of tee shirts and a pair of jeans. An hour later, he called again. This time, a cheerful Ralph answered.

"Yo, it's the Ralph man. What's up?"

"It's Dan again. I will pick you up at nine tomorrow morning. We should miss the city traffic and be on the Jersey Shore by three or before. We can talk on the trip."

"How long am I gone?"

"Don't know. Maybe a week or so." Hughes heard Ralph call out to whoever was there that he would be back in a month or two. "Don't wait."

Giving a weak smile to Angie, he realized he had time to kill and that it may be his last workout for a while. He got out his running shoes, put on shorts and a sweatshirt with the arms cut off, and told Angie he would be back in a couple of hours and left. He headed down the hill in soft-focus sunlight to LA Fitness.

Chapter 25

While Hughes walked toward the looming Ritz Carlton Hotel that housed LA Fitness, Bobby Musa walked out onto the crumbling front porch of his Asbury Park house. He was wearing only workout shorts, and his heavily muscled, deeply tanned chest was an exclamation point of the hot New Jersey summer. He scratched his stomach and watched the few early beachgoers heading for the boardwalk.

Checking his heavy Rolex, he saw he still had two hours before meeting the Syrians. He hated the large Syrian Jewish community of the Shore, but he couldn't pass up the opportunity. They had plenty of money.

He heard scraping noises behind him and he turned to see Arnold looking for something under the couch cushions. Musa suppressed a small smile as he thought of the score he was planning. As best he could figure, Arnold still had a sizable chunk of money left in his trust account. Getting access codes and the right signatures, he could clean it out, buy a huge cache from the Syrians, and turn it over to the Jersey boys for a big profit. If today's meeting went well, he would then call up his contacts and work the sale, keeping a nice skim for himself. All he had to do was keep control of the human wreck he watched through the screen door.

Going back inside, he walked over to Arnold and put his arm around his bony shoulder. "How's my main man?" he asked, barely tolerating the body stink misting off Arnold.

"I'm good, Bobby. But I can't find my wallet. I had some money in it. I need it."

"OK, we'll look together," Musa said, gently pushing Arnold away. "It's probably upstairs. You slept up there last night."

"Oh, yeah. I forgot. I'll look there."

Musa shook his head, thinking that he would only have to tolerate this piggy bank for a little while longer until he could make the big score. Arnold wandered up the rickety stairs and out of sight. Musa looked around at the shambles of the house from the incessant partying and decided he needed a shower.

An hour later, dressed in baggy pants with side pockets and a black muscle shirt, he stepped outside to his Camaro parked in the dirt driveway. Arnold's Mercedes was stashed in the back of the house under a blue plastic tarp. Musa was concerned that the family may have reported it stolen, so he hid it as best as he could. Thinking about it, he decided he would get it over to the chop shop he knew in Bayonne. If nothing else, he could sell it for parts.

He got into the Camaro, and it started with a throaty rumble. Musa sat in it for a minute, listening to it and thinking about how he would be able to trade it in for something classier, like a Maserati. He then drove out and headed for Kelly's, a joint famous for its outrageous Reuben sandwiches and Bloody Marys.

Traffic was surprisingly light as Musa cruised to

Neptune, an indication of summer on the wane. Neptune was a quintessential Shore town, containing tee shirt shops and hot dog stands to satisfy every type of tourist.

Musa parked the Camaro in front, squeezed out of it, and swaggered inside. Even at lunch, the interior was dark, except for the colored lighting around the bar glittering like the remnants of a failed Christmas office party. It took a minute for Musa's eyes to adjust from the glaring August sunshine.

Standing just inside, he looked around for the Syrians. Two were in a back booth, almost out of sight, both dressed in black. Musa recognized Moshe, as thick and square as a dumpster; he didn't know the other guy, a skinny man with a scraggly beard and splotches on his face. He moved cautiously to them and slid in opposite Moshe. Musa tightened like a stretched bungee cord.

"Gentlemen," he said, "how's summer been?"

"Same as always, full of annoying tourists," Moshe mumbled. His voice was surprisingly high and weak, almost feminine.

Turning to the other man, Musa said, "I haven't had the honor."

The man, thin as a reed, did not answer. Moshe simply said he was a friend. Musa gathered he was not to be known.

"I wouldn't think this was your kind of place," Musa said, immediately regretting he said it. Moshe had thick, wet lips like gray leeches that made Musa shudder.

"They're all the same. Cheap."

"OK, let's skip lunch and talk business. OK?" Musa said.

Moshe nodded.

Musa continued, "I am coming into a large sum of

money that I would like to invest. As you may know, I have many contacts in Jersey. If I were to acquire a large amount of product, I could use my contacts to turn it over for a small but decent profit."

Musa glanced around to make sure no one was in earshot. He glanced to his left to the thin man, who exuded a quiet menace. "Even better, no one would be able to know the source of my product. You would be anonymous."

"Why do we need a middleman?" Moshe slurred.

"With respect, I don't believe the end buyers would do business with you." Musa hoped that came over as a non-insult.

The two Syrians were quiet for a minute. Moshe looked at his companion and asked Musa, "How much are we talking about?"

Musa again glanced around. "Maybe pushing a half mil." Arnold, once heavily drugged, had mentioned that sum.

The two men were silent. Musa shifted in the seat and took a breath. Nothing was said for a couple of moments. The smell of frying french fries drifted in from the kitchen. The two Syrians stared at each other, involved in speechless communication. Finally, Moshe spoke. "We can do a deal. We will work out quantity and contact you with a date and place. Understand, we expect very good faith from you."

Despite the air conditioning on full, Musa was sweating. "I won't let you down. This will be good for everybody."

A waitress approached. Without a word, the two men slid out of the booth and walked out of the restaurant, leaving Musa alone and grinning. He threw down a twenty and walked out, ignoring an acquaintance at the bar trying to talk to him.

He got into the Camaro and sat, thinking. Now all he had to do was get the money and set up the deal with the wise guys. He started the powerful car and pointed it back to Asbury Park. The morning mist had burned off, and the noon sun was searingly bright.

Chapter 26

The next morning, a light drizzle blew in from the sea in Boston. The late summer grass on the Boston Common sparkled with the rain like rhinestones.

Hughes did a mental check of what he had packed for the trip. His brown leather duffel was filled with different changes of clothes, binoculars, a miniature tape recorder, and an unloaded .38.

Angie came out of the bathroom in linen shorts and a short-sleeved beige blouse. Her raven hair was pulled back. Hughes smiled. "All set to go?" he asked.

"Ready to go. Adventure is our game. Grab the umbrella. I'll wear my Red Sox cap because of the rain."

"I'll call Ralph and, if he's ready, we can pick him up on the way to get the rental car."

Ralph had a place in a brownstone in the South End, but he was usually with some woman. He always seemed ready to travel light.

Hughes made the call, mildly surprised Ralph answered on the second ring. He was more than ready; he seemed anxious.

After a final look around, he and Angie left the apartment and walked a block to Chestnut Street, where the Mustang was protected from the sun by an enormous tree. They tossed their gear in the trunk and turned onto Joy Street, then down the hill on Beacon. Office workers, soaked from perspiration and the light rain, lined the sidewalks. They turned left onto Charles Street and headed to the South End.

Turning right onto Tremont Street, Hughes spotted Ralph standing in front of the Boston Center of the Arts building. His bald head glistened from the rain, matching the black tee shirt stretching across his chest. He seemed oblivious to the rain. A tiny leather bag was slung over his shoulder. He grinned as they pulled up to the curb.

"Morning, dude," he said, somehow sliding gracefully into the back. His legs were pinched up behind the seat. "I will be a pretzel by the time we reach Jersey."

"Not to worry," Hughes said. We are only going to the Hertz office in Park Square. We will be rolling in style in a big GMC. You can stretch out to your heart's content."

Three minutes later, they pulled up to the parking garage that housed the rental vehicles. After five minutes at the counter, Hughes parked the Mustang in the garage and drove out a shiny black GMC Denali. Ralph looked in at the leather seats and said softly, "Nice ride."

"Glad you approve," Hughes said. He looked at Angie. She smiled and gave up shotgun.

Ralph shrugged. "We get pulled over, a black man in the front seat of this vehicle means you're in cuffs."

"Not with your sparkling personality," Hughes said.

They settled in, bags in the back, and headed for the Mass Pike. At Sturbridge, they turn onto I-84 toward Hartford, and Hughes put the cruise control at seventy.

Ralph stretched. "You got a plan, or are we playing it by ear?"

"We got a plan."

Angie leaned forward from the back seat and asked what it could possibly be, clearly enjoying herself.

"First thing," Hughes said, "I make contact with the locals. Hopefully, I'll find a detective that not only gets it but also is sympathetic. I can't see anything now that's clearly illegal with Arnold. Hard to describe a drug slave. But we are going to try to get him away and hopefully back to his folks and maybe rehab. Then Angie spooks around the group, hopefully staying away from that horny meatball, and tries to find a time that Levine is vulnerable. Then we hustle him into the car and head back to Boston. Simple."

Ralph looked over at him. "Yeah, what could go wrong?"

Angie chuckled from the back seat.

"I'm open to alternative ideas, crack staff."

Ralph and Angie were silent.

As they turned down I-84, Ralph declared a mandatory stop at Rein's Deli. "Best corned beef outside of the city. We must fuel up to save our strength."

Hughes smiled and nodded. Angie rolled her eyes. They sat at the counter, Ralph and Hughes both ordering pastrami on Jewish rye with cream soda, while Angie was content to munch on a giant pickle.

Fortified, they continued south, passing Hartford on the right at a respectable sixty-five miles an hour. When they picked up the Merritt Parkway, Angie and Ralph got into an ongoing conversation about the unique overpasses carved out of the Connecticut woods.

Hughes ignored them, lost in thought. He reviewed what they knew so far, that Arnold was addicted with the help, if not the coercion, of his degenerate keepers. That they were apparently using Arnold's dependency to drain his trust fund. His keepers were not a nice bunch, possibly mob-connected. They would have to be very lucky to be able to get Arnold away from them and back to Boston.

Hughes silently studied his plan without a hint of fear or anxiety. He approached it as he always did, with absolute confidence.

Traffic flowed like migrating salmon, and the Cross Bronx was a clear shot to the George Washington Bridge and across into New Jersey. Hughes had made reservations at a Residence Inn in Neptune, completely unaware of the meeting that had occurred the day before.

After settling in, Angie announced she would like to turn in early, after dinner. Ralph said he was going to spook around to get the lay of the land. Hughes suggested she call the front desk for a dinner recommendation. That recommendation was Kelly's.

They sat at the gaudy bar. Hughes and Ralph, hearing that the restaurant was known for its Bloody Marys, each ordered one. Angie stuck to her chardonnay. Two Reuben sandwiches and a salad later, they settled up. Hughes and Angie retreated to their room, while Ralph took the GMC and headed for Asbury Park for his personal reconnaissance.

The rain had stopped, leaving humidity as thick as fog. Streetlights haloed with an amber glow. It was the quiet before the storm.

Chapter 27

A n ocean breeze blew out the unsettled evening, and the morning woke sparkling bright and fresh.

After showering, Hughes went to check out Ralph, only to find his room empty. Five minutes later, he saw him returning from a punishing five-mile run, dripping with sweat.

Shaking his head, Hughes said, "After the fire department hoses you off, see if Angie wants breakfast. I'm going to the PD to find a sympathetic detective."

Ralph, not even winded, nodded. "Think I'll go to the beach and check out the Jersey talent."

Angie shook her head with a smile. "Be on the lookout for a Tiffany. She's a little pudgy and acts sexy. Can't miss her. She's part of the in-crowd."

"No female is safe from my lookout," Ralph replied.

After calling for directions to the police department, Hughes made his way to a pair of imposing buildings with parking in front. He slid the SUV into a slot for visitors and went into the secured front lobby. It was a cookie cutter of probably every police station in America: a small and somewhat neglected room with a wall of citations and awards with three plastic chairs underneath. Behind a

Plexiglas window, Hughes could see a room containing three desks cluttered with papers and old coffee cups. No officers were seen.

He rang the bell on the side of the window and waited. After a couple of minutes, a muscular officer, his highly starched shirt stretched across a broad chest, approached and politely but indifferently asked if he could help.

Hughes told him he was a private investigator from Boston and needed to talk to a detective. He stared at Hughes for an uncomfortable second. "Wait one," the officer said. "I'll see if Jack is in."

Hughes stood for a couple of minutes with no activity seen or heard. Finally, he settled into a chair as comfortable as a rock and waited.

After a long interval, the officer opened the door on the side and motioned Hughes in. He was led up a flight of stairs to an open room filled with mismatched desks and chairs.

At one desk in the far corner sat a wiry man, apparently in his thirties but with salt-and-pepper hair. He had burly eyebrows and a thick mustache and wore a green Hawaiian-type shirt, untucked. He hung up the phone he was talking on and glared at Hughes, motioning for him to come over. Hughes put on his best professional smile. He stood next to the desk while he was being appraised.

"OK, PI, take a seat and tell me what you want. I'm Jack Ryan," he said, his voice firm and even. Hughes could see a bulge under the shirt.

"My ID," Hughes said, placing his Massachusetts private detective card on the desk. Ryan picked it up, glanced at it, and handed it back. "I'm working on a runaway case. A young man took off and made no effort to let his family know where to find him. It's further complicated by the fact he has a substantial trust fund, which is being drained at an alarming rate."

"Is this guy of legal age?"

"Barely."

"So what's the issue? It's still sort of a free country last time I looked. An adult, even a young one, is allowed to split to parts unknown and is also allowed to spend his own money."

"Right. But right after we found him, we realized he was under the control—pretty much a drug slave—of some not-so-nice people. In fact, when I first started looking, a couple of goons tried to do a tap dance on my face. Looking into it, we are sure they are using drugs on our guy to get him to pull money for them from his trust fund. Sort of larceny by hostage."

Ryan eyed Hughes for a long minute. "So what do you propose you do about this?"

"We are looking to persuade our subject to return to Boston with us so his parents can talk with him. We believe the people who are using him will object to this. Sort of removing the hen laying the golden eggs."

"And is this persuading involving any kind of force?"

Hughes gave a wane smile. "No, we don't do that. But we are concerned our guy's keepers will use force to prevent losing their piggy bank. I just wanted to make you guys aware of us and what we're doing. We're the good guys."

"Who are the bad guys?"

"The one guy we've identified is a guy named Bobby Musa. He seems to be the guy in charge of this."

Ryan was silent. He stared at Hughes. "That name is familiar. Do you know who you are dealing with?"

"Do tell."

"Bobby Musa is an OC wannabe. He tries to rub

shoulders with guys who would eat him up, no matter how tough he thinks he is. Frankly, we would love to find something that would get him out of our hair."

"Whatever we might find, you got it."

Hughes heard voices and footsteps behind him, and he looked around to see two haggard-looking guys wander in and plop down at desks in the far corner. Guys apparently coming in off the night shift. Hughes figured it could not be easy working in the circus that was the Jersey Shore. "Like I said, we're the good guys."

"You here alone?" Ryan continued to give him hard looks. The smell of male sweat filled the room, despite its size.

"I'm here with a female, Angie Carpone, and a black guy, Ralph Lampley. Angie has made direct contact with Musa, who almost raped her. And would've if circumstances were different."

"Not the first time we heard that," Ryan said. "But when it came to bringing charges, all of a sudden none of the women wanted to go forward. Word is that he likes rough sex and likes to rough up women. Like I said, be nice to see the last of him."

"If we call, will the cavalry come running?"

"The black guy your muscle?"

Hughes made a small smile. "I guess so. Never have seen him stand down or go down. Most just stay away from him."

"OK, we met. I'll give some professional courtesy, but only to a limit. If you step in shit, I'll be the first to break your balls, ticket or no ticket from Massachusetts." Ryan turned back to his desk, ending the meeting.

"Thanks, detective. That's all I came here for. And if we

can get anything that will help clean up the beach, you can count on us."

"Just don't fuck up."

* * *

At the beach, Ralph spread a small towel and pulled off his tee shirt. His stretch shorts doubled as a bathing suit. He sat and watched the women strutting back and forth, talking too loudly. After twenty minutes, he got up, stretched, and walked into the water. He found it tepid and oily. After dunking himself, he walked back to his towel, glistening like a seal.

Tiffany was sitting next to it. She looked up at him as he stood, aware of where she was looking. By the look in her eye, he figured this was the infamous Tiffany.

"Hi," she said, grinning. "New here?"

"Yep, just came in from the city. Needed an escape and this seemed as good as any."

"You're right. It's actually better than any." Then standing, her bikini top half off, she said, "Party almost every night. Old gray house with a rickety porch a couple of blocks away. Come by after nine."

He smiled. "How can I find it?"

"Follow the noise," she said over her shoulder as she sauntered away, her string-covered bottom shaking.

He watched her go and thought: "This may be more fun than I thought."

He dusted off the sand and headed back. From the boardwalk, he spotted Angie leaning on the rail and waved.

She waved back and walked to him, marveling at his physique.

When she got close, he whispered, "I met Tiffany."
"Yep, you did. Good work."

* * *

Driving back to the hotel, Hughes considered the meeting and again tried to figure out a plan. The cops did not generate a lot of confidence with their attitude of indifference, and he felt like a stranger in a strange land. As much as he loved the adventures of his job, he always felt like a person watching from the outside, a voyeur instead of a participant.

He passed tourists packing for the beach and sidewalk cafe sitters savoring coffee and the morning papers. Except for himself, it seemed like the world was on holiday. It was a perfect summer day with clear, bright light from a warm sun, and Hughes had his arm out the driver's window as he motored back to the Residence Inn.

As he approached, he saw Ralph and Angie walking along—his thick, powerful body a contrast to her graceful curves. They waved as he drove by them and into the parking lot.

Ralph was wearing a Harley Davidson tee shirt that seemed two sizes too small, and Angie was in white linen shorts with a pale-blue blouse. They made an unusual but attractive couple.

Ralph approached the parking lot as Hughes shut down the GMC. "How did it go with the cops? I see they did not incarcerate you," he said.

"Indifference bordering on annoyance."

Angie rolled her eyes.

"How was the beach?" Hughes asked.

Ralph stretched before answering. "Let's just say I still

got it. Invited to, I think, your den of depravity. So, I'm in without any work at all."

Hughes rolled his eyes.

"So what's the plan?" Ralph asked.

"I think I need a cup of coffee so we can talk about this."

Angie said, "They have some free inside, if there is any left. We can set up camp in the lobby."

"Any port," Hughes responded, already heading for the hotel.

They found a free corner and barely warm coffee still on the coffee bar. Ralph stretched his arms. Two young women in very short shorts and bikini tops stopped to stare at him. Angie rolled her eyes again. Hughes grinned.

"OK," Ralph said. "What have you gotten me into? If nothing is going to happen soon, I am heading to the beach."

"Got a bathing suit?" Angie asked.

"Don't need one, I hear."

"Yeah, if you don't mind throwing women into a frenzy."

Hughes took a sip of his coffee and winced. "Let's focus here. What I'm thinking is we watch the group until we see Levine alone. We put him in the car and head to Boston."

"That's your plan?" Ralph laughed. "Why don't we just ask him to take the bus home? What about his minders? Think they will go along with that?"

"Got a better idea?" Hughes watched two other women barely dressed for the beach walk out.

Angie stared at Hughes and thought for a minute. "I know what we should do, Danny. I can go back into the lion's den and see if there is ever a time he's alone. From there, we can work out what to do."

Hughes was silent for a moment. "I don't want you to go near that animal, but I don't know what else we can do. Think you can handle that asshole?"

"I've handled bigger assholes," she replied, pushing her coffee cup far away on the coffee table.

Ralph shrugged. "I can wait in the shadows and be on asshole alert for her. I would never let anything happen to my Angie. But since I've already got an invitation, maybe it's better if I go in."

"The only thing we can do is spook around and see what might work. Ninety percent of the solution is identifying the problem."

"OK, great sage," Angie laughed. "Let's get going."

Ralph groaned, "No more beach for the working class. All those women will be disappointed."

Standing, Angie said, "Might disappoint them but will save humiliation of their boyfriends unable to compare."

Ralph nodded, and they walked back out into the warming day.

They motored at a slow pace back to Asbury Park. It was already feeling like summer was on the wane. The town was busy but without the enthusiasm evident in the middle of July. They watched the scene from the windows of the SUV, silently thinking their own thoughts.

Chapter 28

usa looked at his Rolex and saw that it was two o'clock. He figured it was a little early to contact Barcinko with his scheme. He pulled into the dirt driveway next to the house and saw Tiffany sitting on the front porch, her legs up on the banister. Arnold was in a tattered straw chair next to her, pale as paper.

Musa got out of the car and walked up the front steps. He saw that Tiffany was holding a bottle of tequila in one hand and a glass in another. As he watched, she poured about a third of a glass and handed it to Arnold. He took it without a word and took a sip. Musa shook his head in disgust. He saw Tiffany was wearing bikini bottoms under a dirty tee shirt. The bottoms barely covered her crotch and part of her labia was out on one side.

"Trying to get arrested?" Musa hissed at her.

"What?"

"What? Your pussy is hanging out. Didn't notice you were getting stares from people?"

Tiffany grinned. Musa realized she was already drunk.

"You're supposed to be taking care of my pal Arnie." To him, "How you doin', buddy?"

Arnold nodded in a drugged state.

"Screw you, Bobby," Tiffany slurred. "You made me stay here while you're running around, probably with some bimbos."

Musa stared at her. "Get your ass inside. I have to talk with Arnie."

She got up in a huff, spilling her drink on the coffee table and stomped off through the front door. Musa pulled her chair up to Arnold and patted him on the shoulder. "You doin' OK?"

Arnold gave him a small smile, and Musa saw he was pretty well gone. Lowering his voice, he said, "We need to make a big score, and when I do, we can get out of this place and go down to the islands where no one knows us. Want to do that?"

Arnold stared with glassy eyes. "That would be good, Bobby. Everyone here treats me like shit."

"It means I need to borrow what you have left. With the investment I'm making, I'll be able to pay you right back."

A car horn blew, and Arnold stared toward the road. Musa was unsure if he understood anything he had just said but figured he'd get what he wanted when the time came. He patted Arnold on the shoulder and got up and went into the house, looking for Tiffany. He saw her sprawled out on the couch, asleep. Shaking his head, he went through the house and into the backyard. He pulled out a piece of paper with a phone number on it and punched the number into his cell phone. The call was answered on the third ring.

"Yeah."

"Is this Vinnie?"

No answer.

"I would like to talk to Mr. Barcinko."

"You want to talk, come to our place."

"When?"

The call was terminated. Musa stood thinking. Hated to, but he would have to see Barcinko face to face again.

He went back inside and found Tiffany sitting up, a blank look in her eyes. He could see Arnold still sitting on the front porch, inert. Tiffany looked much older than she was, and Musa felt disgusted. She was even beginning to look out of place with the other girls in their twenties.

"Get yourself cleaned up. I need you to babysit tonight," he said, gesturing with his head to Arnold on the porch.

"Aw, Bobby. There's a new group at the Pony. I wanted to go there tonight. All the girls will be there." She was shaking off her nap and rubbing her eyes.

"You'll fuckin' do what I want you to fuckin' do," he replied sharply.

She recoiled from his words.

"I got to go some place. Be gone about two hours or so. You will be here and watch over my guy Arnie. Capisce?"

She tugged at her tee shirt. "OK, Bobby, if you say so. Anything special I should do?"

"Feed my boy and clean this place up. It looks like a shithole."

"What do I feed him?" Her voice was a whisper.

Musa rolled his eyes. She was stupider than he thought.

Musa tossed two twenties on the end table. "Order up pizzas. I don't want him going out. So stay here with him. Play Monopoly or some fucking thing."

"OK, Bobby," she said meekly, picking up the money and sticking it down on the side of her bikini bottom.

Musa glared at her, then headed upstairs to change and clean up. He chose his best white silk shirt with black slacks and his dark-blue running shoes. He made sure the gold around his neck stood out as he surveyed himself in the dirty mirror. *I will make this deal and get rid of creepy Levine. Maybe move to St. Barts,* he thought to himself and smiled.

Downstairs, he heard Tiffany call to Arnold to come inside. He would have to closely watch the quantity of dope he was giving to Arnold. *Don't want him to OD before I get this done.*

By five o'clock, he headed to the Wonder Bar, nervous about the meeting with the boys in Jersey City. The bar was almost empty with a few of the beachgoers starting to drift in. There was a group on the back patio; by the sound of them, they must have been there for a while. Musa glanced out and, recognizing no one, ignored them and ordered a Patron shooter at the bar. As he was throwing it down, Stubby McConnell, a Shore burnout Musa knew from the scene, came in and waved to him. Musa nodded back.

McConnell came over. "Hi, Bobby. What's up?"

"Not much." Then he thought for a minute. "Stubby, what do you know about the Syrian Jews on the Shore?"

"Bad fuckers. I stay away from them."

"Can you trust them?"

"Trust them to do what? Pick your pocket? They'd sell you a jackass and call it Secretariat."

Musa was quiet. Finally, "OK, thanks." He worried about his scheme and signaled for another shooter.

Forty minutes later, he climbed into the Camaro and headed north. Traffic on the Parkway was heavy southbound but fairly light going north. He was entering Jersey City as the last light of day faded into purple dusk.

A series of lefts and rights brought him to the cinder block bar he knew was the unofficial headquarters of some made men. He parked to the side and took a deep breath.

Pulling open the solid front door, he realized it was steel-reinforced. He pulled it open and squinted into the dark interior.

A large man, heavy in the shoulders with a large overhanging belly, stood at the far end of the bar. He had a pockmarked face and a sad comb-over. He eyed Musa suspiciously. Musa figured he was a bodyguard. His eyes adjusting, he saw two men at a corner table and recognized them as Vinnie and Barcinko. He stood and waited for a gesture to approach. They stared at him. Finally, Vinnie wiggled his finger at him.

Musa walked to the table and stood, waiting. Both men looked up at him with hostility. Vinnie had a thin mustache that was like a black worm on his upper lip. His eyes were a cold December night. Sour body odor rose from both men. Finally, Barcinko indicated with a nod that Musa could sit.

"Hello, Mr. Barcinko, Vinnie," Musa said uncertainly.

"What the fuck do you want?" Barcinko's words came out in a hiss.

"I'm about to score a big hit of H. Was wondering if you guys would want to buy at a big discount."

Barcinko and Vinnie looked at each other. "Do tell," Vinnie said.

"I can get you $800K of product at $700K. Top grade. Can be stepped on two, maybe three times."

Vinnie laughed. "How the fuck does a beach rat get that kind of bread? You figure out a stupid Internet scam? Illusions of grandeur."

"Look, I've been buying from you guys every month. You know I'm good for it. I'm going to cash out my piggy bank and toss it away. Turn the capital into an investment. Works out for all of us. Except, of course, my piggy bank."

Barcinko and Vinnie sat quietly. Finally, Vinnie said, "You buying from the kikes? We don't do business with them."

"I know. But you'll be doing business with me. I'm almost family."

"Maybe someday in your dreams. Get your product and let us know about the deal. We'll see then," Barcinko whispered. "We'll do the deal when it's set. One time only. You better be sure."

The large man at the end of the bar shifted on his feet and made a deep sound in his throat. Musa looked over at him, unsure. Barcinko gestured with his head an all-clear. The dumpster at the end of the bar turned back to his drink.

"Nothing comes back to us," Barcinko said. "You fuck this up, we fuck you up."

"The phone number still good?" Musa asked, his voice nervously cracking.

Vinnie nodded and turned back to face Barcinko, signaling the meeting was over. Musa nodded, got up, and made his way to the door. He felt the eyes from the end of the bar follow him out.

He got into the Camaro and let out a long sigh. *Now all I have to do is clean out Levine's account, make him disappear, and buy the product from the Syrians. These guys will make money, and I'll get respect. Not far from a home run.*

He pulled a small paper from his wallet. On it was a series of numbers. The password to Arnold's trust fund. Studying the numbers, he congratulated his brilliance. He'd transfer Arnold's money to an account the Syrians gave him and get the dope from them. He'd then tell Barcinko he was ready to go and meet them, sell the junk at a hundred-grand profit, and take the next flight to St. Barts. Arnold would be collateral damage.

Chapter 29

Motoring to Asbury Park, the three were silent in the large and heavy car.

Angie watched the sunbaked stores and diners supporting the summer crowd go by, thinking it could be fun just to be on vacation like normal people. Ralph closed his eyes and went totally inert. It was hard to tell if he was awake or asleep.

Hughes kept running over his plan in his mind. Not a good plan but he couldn't come up with anything else. If Arnold fought them or if his minders interfered, they would come out with nothing. But according to Angie, Arnold was on his last legs, and if he weren't taken out of there soon, he never would be. They cruised by The Stone Pony, which, closed during the day, looked like an abandoned warehouse. Then they passed Musa's house, which looked equally empty.

There was no car in the driveway, and Hughes wondered about the Mercedes that Arnold supposedly drove. A blue tarp covered something in the back. Probably it. He wondered if they could get it back to Boston but then figured it would only complicate things. Maybe get it later.

Only one drive-by could be risked, so they parked the car two blocks away and walked back, trying to look casual as they strolled past on the broken sidewalk. A dirt pathway ran along the side of the house, leading to the street behind. Behind the house was a littered and desolate backyard. Along its side was an ancient stockade fence, falling down. One of the sections of the fence had several boards broken, producing a hole large enough to squeeze through.

Looking into the yard, they saw a couple of plastic chairs and a chaise lounge, half-rusted. They kept on walking and circling around back to their rental car.

"If we can get Arnold into the backyard, we can drive the car down along the fence, go in, and pull him out. Once in the car, all we have to do is drive back to Boston," Hughes speculated.

Ralph gave him a look.

Angie rolled her eyes. "Why don't we just ask him to take the bus back?" she said sarcastically.

"Don't have any better ideas. We'll tell the cops we are going to try to take Levine back without telling them how. Ask them to be around if there's any trouble," Hughes said. "Let's get out of here before someone spots us."

No one came up with any better ideas on the ride back.

Finally, Angie said, "You have some expense money. I suggest you use it to buy us a good meal."

Ralph nodded. "You got that right."

"OK, how about Italian?"

* * *

Musa drove from Jersey City to a rundown neighborhood in Newark. After searching around a few blocks, he found the building he was looking for. It was a gray, boarded-up box that once housed a small grocery store, long abandoned. There was a bicycle chained to a post with its rear wheel missing.

Musa parked on the side and sat for a minute, checking out the area in his car mirrors. Satisfied, he got out of the car and locked it. Looking around, he went to the graffiti-stained door and knocked. Nothing. He knocked again and heard a shuffling from inside. He leaned into the door and said, "It's Bobby Musa from Asbury Park. You know me."

After a minute, the door opened a crack but was held fast by an inside chain. Sullen and bloodshot eyes peered out at him. The chain was finally dropped and the door was opened. Standing inside was a thin thirty-year-old going on fifty. His sparse hair was pulled over into an obvious comb-over. There were red blotches on his face. Despite the heat, he was wearing bib overalls with no shirt underneath. Musa stepped inside to an apparent flophouse, and the door was closed.

"Haven't seen you in a while," he said to Musa.

"Sorry, Mud. I had to use another source for the day-to-day stuff."

"So what do you want?"

"I need something special. Something that will be the last thing used."

The man called Mud looked at him without talking. Finally, he said, "I don't know from nothing."

"Of course, but I've got five hundred here that will ensure I was never here."

Mud stared at him, then turned, and walked to a steel, scratched desk in the corner. He unlocked a drawer and turned back to Musa. "I have a syringe that has H, coke, and a hint of antifreeze. A former client was going to use it on a racehorse, then changed his mind. I call it the Pearly Gates. Is that what you are looking for?"

"Yeah."

"A thousand."

Musa glared at him for a long minute, then pulled out a wad of money and counted out the thousand. He thought that was cheap for an OD and a green light to grab that money. He turned and walked out, saying as he left, "You don't know nuthin.'"

He put the wrapped syringe on the passenger seat and looked at it with a small amount of dread. He headed back to Asbury Park feeling God-like.

* * *

Back in Red Bank, Hughes led them to Anthony's. Striding into the cool interior, he looked for Annie Treat. Behind the bar instead was a middle-aged man dressed in a blue button-down shirt and khaki slacks. He seemed fit and happy, greeting the group as they entered.

"Annie working tonight?" Hughes asked.

"No, you got me instead. Annie's got the night off. I think she has a date."

"Lucky guy," Hughes said. "Well, we're hungry and have somewhere to go a little later. Got something fast and good?"

The only ones at the bar, they settled in at the far corner. Menus were brought to them, along with water and a large basket of freshly baked bread. Hughes pushed the wine list aside. "Let's keep a very clear head," he said.

Hughes and Ralph ordered pasta with meatballs, Angie a salad with Italian dressing. As they ate, the bartender found other customers at the other end, giving them a fair amount of privacy.

"I would probably be known but, Ralph, you've met Tiffany before, so you can drift in and look like you're looking for some action. Angie, you take the wheel and place the car at the end of the side street. I'll ride over with you and get out and go to the opening in the fence. Ralph, if somehow you can get Levine into the backyard, I'll help you get him out through the fence. I'll run interference if necessary. Once you get him into the car, take off. I'll be behind you on foot and head for the boardwalk, where there will be a lot of people. Swing around and see if you see me. If not, head for Boston. I'll find a way."

Angie looked at him like he was crazy. "Find a way? How far can you hitchhike?"

"On the way over, I'm calling the cops. I'll tell Detective Ryan we are taking Levine back to Boston. I'll ask if they can be on the lookout for us. If I'm stuck afterward, I'll call him and see if he can give me a ride to the train station."

Ralph was quiet and munched on a meatball. After a minute, he said, "That's a shitty plan. A million things can go wrong. You're assuming the house will be mostly empty and Levine will be there. I don't see him helping us remove him and into an unknown car."

"If he is, get him out and through the fence, even if you have to carry him. If you go in and it doesn't look like you can do that, send a text. Just say 'no go' and we'll pick you up down the street in ten minutes."

Ralph looked toward two women at a table and nodded. They finished the meals mostly in silence.

It grew misty dark as Hughes paid the bill and they headed out. He told the bartender to say hello to Annie for him, and he got a leering grin back. Angie got behind the wheel with Hughes in front and Ralph comfortably lounging in the back seat. She drove slowly south to Asbury Park.

Meanwhile, Musa returned from Newark, parking his powerful car in the dirt driveway next to the house. He held the wrapped syringe in his left hand like he was holding a live snake.

Entering the living room, he saw no one. He called out to Arnold and heard a faint shuffling coming from the kitchen. He half-smiled to himself. He walked into the kitchen and saw Arnold making a sandwich out of white bread and some slimy pieces of ham.

"What's happening, Arnie, my man?" he asked. Arnold looked at him with glazed eyes.

Shit, Musa thought to himself. *He's almost gone already. Won't take much to finish the job.*

He figured he would wait for the right time and then give Arnold the shot. It would take only seconds for him to OD and for his lights to go out.

Chapter 30

A soft dusk was settling over the resort area as they made their way to Asbury Park. Hughes took out his cell phone and the business card he got from Detective Ryan. He punched in the number and waited. Surprisingly, the call was answered after two rings.

"Ryan." The voice sounded like a piece of paper tearing.

"Detective, this is Dan Hughes, the PI from Boston."

Silence.

"Detective? Remember me?"

"I suspect you are going to be a pain in the ass."

"Course not. Just want to let you know we are going to ask Levine to come back to his folks tonight if we can find him."

"Find him where?"

"We know he's living in that house where Bobby Musa lives, so we are going there."

Again, silence.

"So what do you need from me?"

"Just want to let you know in case something gets ugly."

"We don't care about runaways. The Jersey Shore is littered with them. Do what you do; just stay away from the law."

Hughes listened quietly, then he heard, "Just don't fuck up."

The call terminated.

Hughes turned and looked back at Ralph. "That was not encouraging," he said.

"Cops never are," Ralph replied, staring out the side window.

"OK," Hughes said. "We have a plan. Let's give it a try."

Ralph said, "Tell me again why I am in the house?"

"The usual. Looking for tail."

Angie glanced over at Hughes and rolled her eyes.

The trip from Red Bank to Asbury Park took thirty-five minutes. As they pulled into town, darkness had taken hold. The streetlights were haloed with a yellow glow. People were out, heading to restaurants and making early visits to the bars and clubs.

As they traveled down Ocean Avenue, they could see strollers on the boardwalk, soft-focus figures in the growing mist. They passed The Stone Pony, closed and looking like a cold and empty warehouse, then turned right onto First Street. They rode by the house without looking but could see lights were on, and the Camaro was parked on the side. As they drove by, a black Ford sedan, with two guys who looked like they were wearing Hawaiian shirts inside, cruised by in the other direction. Angie and Hughes looked at each other, wondering if the cops were around. They saw no one was on the porch, and no sounds came from the inside.

Angie drove smoothly for two blocks and then pulled to the side. She looked over at Hughes and waited. They said nothing for a couple of minutes. The soft din from the crowds could be heard, but inside the car, it was completely silent. Finally, Hughes told Ralph it was time to take a look inside the house, making sure his and Angie's numbers were on his speed dial.

"I'm on it, boss," Ralph replied and climbed out of the car. He paused next to it and surveyed the area. The air was thick. He smiled back at Hughes and Angie and started toward the house. Hughes told Angie to drive slowly to the side road next to the fence.

Inside the house, Musa went upstairs to the chaos of his bedroom. He pulled out an old running shoe from the closet. Stashed inside was the syringe wrapped in newspaper. He unwrapped and inspected it. Didn't seem possible death could reside in such a small package. Although Musa had talked tough, this was a major step for him. But he felt Arnold was nothing more than a rich piece of human garbage and wouldn't be missed. Musa would lie low for a while in St. Barts, enjoying paradise, then head back when things cooled. Although the money was good, he knew that by doing this deal, he would be seen much differently by the Jersey City boys. He would be on his way to becoming a soldier in the mob, maybe leading to being made. This was the beginning of the big time.

Musa heard the door open behind him, and he quickly stuck the needle in the dresser drawer. Turning, he saw Tiffany sleepily smiling at him. She was wearing a stained sweatshirt and what appeared to be bikini bottoms. Her makeup was smeared and her hair was a mangled nest.

"Bobby, where have you been? I've missed you," she breathed.

He glared back at her. "Business. Get yourself cleaned up. You look like trash."

"Bobby, don't be that way. I just got up."

"Just got up? It's nine-thirty at night."

"I know, but we partied on the beach. Can't remember much after four o'clock."

Musa had to get her out of the way. But first, he had to deal with Arnold. His plan was to transfer Arnold's funds into the Syrians' account, then get him outside in the back, give him the needle, and wait an hour or so before discovering him and calling the EMT. That way, he would be sure Arnold was gone before meeting the Syrians. Once the transfer was complete, he'd call Vinnie and set up a meet an hour after getting the dope from the Syrians. About five hours that would change his life.

"Go clean yourself up. We can talk later."

"Oh, Bobby," she said, coming up to him. "Let me make you happy. It's been so long."

He felt revulsion but needed her to back up his story of Arnold being a hopeless junkie on his own. "Later, baby," he said, putting his arm around her. Her flesh was soft and spongy from too much excess. "I will make both of us happy." He gave her more of a grimace than a smile. She sighed and put her head on his shoulder. He could smell sour breath.

"OK, baby. Whenever you want."

He pulled away. "OK, babes, I've got some work to do. You clean up and relax. We'll hook up a little later."

She looked up at him with doe eyes, nodded, and then shuffled back out of the room.

Musa took the syringe out of the drawer and looked at it again, holding it gingerly.

Ralph, at the same time, was making his way to the front porch of the house. He looked up to the lighted windows and listened. It was quiet. He made his way to the front door and knocked. No answer. He tried the doorknob, and it gave way easily. He peered into the living room.

There were two table lamps lit, but no one could be seen. He let himself in, calling out. After a minute, he heard Tiffany descending the stairs. She stopped at the bottom and grinned at him.

"Hi, dude. I remember you. What can I do for you?" she said.

"No party tonight?" he asked. "Just looking for some more action."

Tiffany ran a hand across her mouth and glanced upstairs for Musa. "Stick around; something should happen," she said.

"Anybody around?" he asked innocently.

"Bobby's upstairs, and Arnie's around somewhere. I'm around." The hint obvious.

"OK, I'll hang out," Ralph said, glancing toward the kitchen where he heard some dim noise.

Tiffany leered at him. "I'm going upstairs to shower. Be back in no time. Stick around."

Ralph grinned at her. "I'll be here." He was thinking it could not be better. As Tiffany turned and waddled up the stairs, he went to the kitchen and found it empty. He looked out the back door and saw Arnold lying in a chaise in the derelict backyard. He stepped to the side and pulled out his cell phone. Looking around, he sent a text saying, "Go, go."

Hughes read the text and felt the adrenaline flow. He told Angie to drive opposite the opening in the fence and get ready to move out. He jumped out of the car and made his way along the fence to the opening. Peering inside, he saw Arnold in the chaise from a different angle. He could see the outline of Ralph in the back doorway.

Upstairs, Musa sat in front of his computer, where he had made the transfer to the Syrians' account. He knew there would be a verification request coming back in minutes, and he was ready with the password he had gotten from Arnold before.

He dialed a number on his cell phone, getting a recording he knew was the Syrians. He left a message: "Check your account and go behind the Sandy Dunes Diner in an hour." He knew the diner would be closed, that it would be dark behind it, and they would be out of sight from the road.

Then he placed a call to the number he had for Vinnie and Barcinko. A hollow recorded voice said to leave a message. Musa said, "The deal is ready to go down. One a.m. behind the Sandy Dunes Diner. I'll transfer a duffel bag with the product to you. Guarantee it's good. In and out in thirty seconds. He punched the call off and grinned. Everything was in place.

In the bathroom next to Musa's room, Tiffany stepped out of the shower feeling better. Drying herself with a towel, she walked out of the bathroom and into the second bedroom. She was thinking Ralph would make a nice addition to the fun.

As she toweled off her hair, she looked out the rear window. Nothing she saw registered at first. She spotted Arnold sprawled out on the chaise, then was startled to see a large, dark figure dash out the back door and grab him. Still unsure what she was seeing, she dropped the towel and yelled out. "What are you doing? Leave him alone!" Then, "Bobby, they're grabbing Arnie," she screamed.

Ralph heard the scream from the open window but ignored her. Musa also heard and looked out, seeing what Tiffany saw. At first not comprehending, he then grabbed the syringe with animal cunning and rushed to go down the stairs. He banged out the back door, just as Ralph was frog-marching Arnold out through the fence.

Hughes was standing just inside the yard. "Go, Ralph!" he screamed. "Go!"

As Ralph dragged Arnold through the fence and into the back seat of the SUV, Hughes stood his ground as Musa charged him.

"You! You!" Musa screamed as he recognized Hughes and saw Arnold disappearing out of sight. He charged at Hughes and brought the needle up to stab him with it. Hughes danced to the side and, bringing his hands up, lashed out with a right that struck Musa in his mouth, splitting his lip. Musa staggered back a half-step, tasted the blood in his mouth, and roared with anger. Hughes danced backward, looking for an escape. He steeled himself to battle a much larger man.

Musa shook with anger, his eyes as wide as the white marbles back in the Levines' Boston townhouse. He picked up a steel bar that was left over from a broken chair and again came at Hughes. He still had the needle in one hand and the bar held high in the other. Hughes stepped back and to the side. He held his arms up to defend against the blow that would surely break something.

Suddenly, from the corner of his eye, he saw a dark flash. Ralph had stormed through the fence, a charging stallion. He stepped in front of Musa, his fists flying like jackhammers, blasting into Musa in heavy one-two successions. Then he gave a penetrating kick to his ribs. Musa fell back and down, stunned, the steel bar flying. Ralph grabbed Hughes by his arm and pulled him into the gap in the fence; the waiting SUV Angie was behind the wheel of was ready to go. Hughes jumped into the front seat and Ralph, into the back.

"Go!" Hughes yelled, and Angie hit the gas. Gravel spewed as the heavy vehicle got traction and flew down the dirt pathway and out onto the street.

Musa jumped up, shook his head, and ran to his Camaro, next to the path in the driveway. Tossing the deadly needle on the passenger seat, he pulled the key from his pocket, started the car, and roared out onto the street in pursuit. He saw the black SUV, just hundreds of yards ahead, sail down the street and turn left onto Ocean. He accelerated, flying past slower vehicles on the road, passing on the left.

Ahead, Hughes turned around in his seat and saw the Camaro coming after them. He told Angie to speed up. Holding both hands on the wheel, Angie held the SUV firm. She was shaking from the effort.

"We've got to get Levine away from here and somehow away from that animal," Hughes said to her. She increased the speed. Glancing at Arnold, she saw his head roll uncomprehendingly.

As they rounded a curve, unbelievably, blue-flashing lights appeared behind them. Police. How fast was she going? Fast. No choice but to pull over. She did and the police sedan, its lights making odd reflections on the beach houses, pulled in behind. Both cars clicked and snapped as they cooled.

Ryan climbed out of the passenger side and another muscular man out from behind the wheel. Both were wearing loud Hawaiian shirts, untucked, right hands on their hips. Ryan came to the side window and looked at Hughes with mild amusement. He looked into the back seat and saw Ralph sitting next to a dazed Arnold Levine. Ralph gave him a small smile.

Just as Ryan was going to say something, Musa came

roaring up the boulevard in the Camaro. With the SUV and the police sedan partially blocking the road, he slammed on his brakes, bringing his car into a skid. Unable to completely stop, he bashed into the police car, knocking it sideways. Ryan and his partner looked back in disbelief.

"Don't fucking move," Ryan said to Hughes. "I'll be back for you when I deal with this asshole."

Inside the SUV, the group watched the two detectives go to either side of the Camaro. Musa still sat stupidly at the wheel. Ryan yanked the driver's door open and grabbed Musa by his shoulder and hair. He pulled him out of the car and pushed him up against it. Stretching Musa's arms behind, Ryan cuffed him while his partner looked inside the coupe. He reached under the front seat and found a Glock 16. He grinned.

Cars were backing up on the road, and some people came out on the porches of their beach houses to watch. Ignoring the gathering crowd, Ryan spun Musa around, recognizing him. "Mr. Musa, I presume," he said sarcastically. "I was wondering when I would get to you up close and personal."

Musa could only think of the meetings he had scheduled and the verification he had to give to authorize the transfer of the funds. Ryan and the other officer walked him to the cruiser and pushed him into the back seat.

As they were shoving his large head down into the car, a black Lincoln sedan with blacked-out windows silently coasted by, maneuvering around the other cars in the road and onlookers. Inside, Vinnie, behind the wheel, and Barcinko, in the back, looked out at the scene on the road. They watched Musa seated in the back, staring blankly ahead.

"Asshole," Barcinko said.

Vinnie nodded and accelerated away and toward the Parkway.

Detective Ryan walked back to the SUV where Hughes, Angie, and Ralph sat watching. Arnold had his eyes closed and was inert as a pillar.

"Out," Ryan commanded Hughes. "The rest of you stay where you are."

Hughes got out of the car and started to speak. Ryan cut him off.

"What the fuck is going on, hotshot?"

"We are taking the runaway back to Boston. The guy you have in your car apparently didn't like that idea. He was chasing us, and we believe he's dangerous."

Ryan looked back at the SUV and thought. "You are probably right about the dangerous part. We've been looking for a reason to take him down for a long time. We've now got something on him with the weapon and apparently some dope. At least enough to cool him down some. Tell me more about the stiff you've got in the back seat with that big black guy."

"We are sure some people, like the guy you've got in your car, were doping him up and, while he was totally stoned, they were draining his trust fund. From what we see, he needs immediate medical attention to try to dry him out. We are bringing him back to his folks."

"How old is that guy?" Ryan asked, still staring at the SUV.

"He's nineteen."

Ryan called over to his partner. "Bill, get the broad and the black guy out of the car and bring them here." To Hughes, "You, PI, stay right here while I sort this out." Hughes nodded.

The other detective went to the SUV and told Angie and Ralph to get out and lean against the car. They did and he patted them down and then walked them to where Ryan and Hughes stood. By this time, a good-sized crowd had developed and stood watching. Then a marked police cruiser pulled up behind; two uniforms got out and walked over. One of them called to Ryan, "Jack, need help?"

Ryan shook his head, then told them, "Just keep an eye on these three. We've got one in back that is going in. Maybe four more." He then walked to the SUV where Arnold still sat, now looking around confused. He opened the door and stuck his head in and took in Arnold for a long minute. Then he said, "Sir, are you all right?"

It took a bit for Arnold to understand; then he looked through the rear window at the scene on the street and Musa dimly visible in the back of the unmarked sedan. He then nodded his head up and down.

"I'm all right, but I'm hungry," he whispered.

Ryan stared at him. "Sir, are you with those people voluntarily? They say they are taking you back to Boston."

Arnold was silent. Ryan waited, then said, "Sir, do you understand what I've just said?"

After a minute, Arnold said, "I'm OK. I want to go home." The words came from a deep inner cave of anguish and despair.

Ryan pushed. "Do you mean your home in Boston?"

Arnold's eyes welled up. Then he said, "Yes, I want to leave this place."

Ryan studied him for a few moments more, then, shaking his head, walked back to the waiting group. He said to Hughes, "Get the fuck out of my town and don't come back. That kid's in tough shape. Maybe you are doing the right thing. I don't know. But I can't figure anything to hold you on. So I'm telling you to get the hell off the Jersey Shore without breaking any laws."

He turned to his partner and said, "Let's run Musa in and figure out what he was going to do with the piece he had under the seat. Send that nasty-looking needle over to the lab for analysis. I think I have an idea of what he was going to do with it." Then, turning to the two uniforms, "Get the traffic moving again and get these people back to where they came from."

With that, he got into the front seat of the sedan. He turned around and grinned at Musa. Musa just stared out the side window.

Angie and Ralph looked at Hughes. He glanced around, smiled, and shrugged. "Angie, you can still drive and, Ralph, you sit with Levine. Let's go slow and steady to win this race."

Without further words, they got back into the SUV. Angie started it, put it into gear, and slowly drove north.

From the front passenger seat, Hughes turned to Arnold, who had his eyes closed again. "Arnie," he said, "we've got a long ride ahead. We'll do a pit stop pretty soon, but right now I want to take the advice of the police officer and get out of here. OK?"

Arnold was quiet.

From Red Bank, they picked up the Garden State. Traffic was light because of the late hour. They pulled over at the first rest stop and brought a burger and fries out to Arnold, who sat in the car motionless. He was sweating heavily. Angie put her hand on his forehead and found him very warm. She looked at Hughes with alarm and urged him to get going. Hughes got behind the wheel and continued the ride to Boston with her in the back with Arnold and Ralph in shotgun.

They continued smoothly, running across the George Washington Bridge, the city twinkly below like the crystals of a chandelier. They headed north and followed the opposite route they had taken to the Shore just a day ago. It seemed like weeks to Hughes. He drove at just above the speed limit, stopping only once again for gas. Again, Arnold remained in back, apparently asleep.

Dawn was glowing orange in the east as they made it into Boston and picked up heavy commuter traffic going in.

Angie sleepily looked out her window and said quietly, "I wonder what's it like to be completely normal?"

Ralph turned back to her and replied, "Not fun. This is better."

They got off the Mass Pike Extension at Prudential and swung around to Marlboro Street. Hughes double-parked in front of the Levines' townhouse. The leafy street seemed too perfect to be true. No pedestrians were seen in the early morning light, and some of the outside entrance lights were still on, casting deep shadows.

Hughes got out and opened the back door. He reached in and took Arnold's arm. "Come on, Arnie. We are going to say hello to your folks."

Arnold looked confused but slid out without resistance. Still holding his arm, Hughes walked him up to the front door and banged on the door knocker. Nothing happened; Hughes knocked twice again. Finally, the door opened a crack, and Hughes could see the thick glasses of Ira peering out. Then the door pulled all the way open, and Ira stood wearing what appeared to be a full-length dressing gown. His mouth hung open.

"Here he is," Hughes said. "I take no responsibility for his condition."

Arnold looked like he had just climbed out of a coffin.

"Oh my god," Ira muttered. "Sara, wake up! Arnold is home." Shuffling could be heard upstairs. "How can we ever thank you?"

Hughes smiled tiredly. "I'll send you a bill tomorrow. In the meantime, I would strongly urge you to call a doctor."

Sara appeared like a tugboat covered with billowing cotton. She glared at Arnold through squinted eyes. "Get in here," she hissed. With that, she grabbed him by his arm and yanked him inside.

Ira's eyes welled up. He shrugged to Hughes and closed the door. After a minute, Hughes turned and walked slowly back to the car, where Angie and Ralph were waiting. "Let's go home," he whispered. "It's been a long day."

Chapter 31

A breeze from the sea filtered through the high buildings, bringing with it a hint of fall. It was still warm but not as humid as just a week ago. The Red Sox looked they would make the playoffs, and the city braced for the end of the summer respite.

Hughes walked to the back of Beacon Hill, where he had parked the Mustang. He took in deep breaths, feeling a new energy. Pulling off the parking ticket stuck under the windshield wiper, he tossed it onto the floor of the car as he climbed in. Then he started the convertible and opened the top.

As it was settling into the rear well, a thirtysomething blonde wearing a cherry-red dress and sensible heels walked by. She paused and smiled at Hughes. He smiled back. After an instant flirt, she continued up the hill and he shifted into first.

He slowly motored through Back Bay and to the curb in front of Abe & Louie's. The valet standing in front ran to the car and opened the driver's door. "Leave it in front?" he said to Hughes.

"You bet," Hughes replied and stepped out of the car

and to the front entrance. Inside, as usual, Mario stood at the top of the short entrance stairs. He grinned at Hughes.

"Lots of bad guys here tonight. Cougar night, you know. We had a film crew in here last Thursday and had to put a sign out front alerting guys that video was being shot. Bar business fell thirty percent."

"I'll duck under a table if I see anyone with a camera," Hughes chuckled. "Can I do the usual, table for two outside in about forty-five minutes?"

"Shouldn't be a problem. I'll let you know when it's ready. Enjoy the evening." Hughes wasn't sure if the excellent service was because of healthy tips, frequent visits, or just excellent service. He made his way to the bar, which was half-empty because of the early hour. True to Mario's comment, there were four cougars cruising and two suits. Mike, a jukebox with feet, spotted him and ambled over.

"Hey, super sleuth," he offered for a greeting. "Should be a fair amount of predators in here tonight. I'd be careful."

"You got that right. Angie is going to show up soon. Protect me."

Mike laughed. "What can I get you?"

"Let's do the Ketel One martini, made the Mike way."

"Coming right up." He moved away and started mixing the drink.

Hughes glanced around and made eye contact with a forty-year-old woman going on thirty-three a couple of stools away. He returned her smile, gave it a fleeting thought, and turned away. She understood the body language and also turned back. Dusk settled over the city like a silk robe.